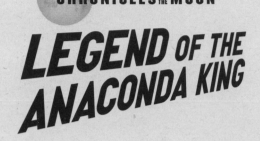

CHRONICLES OF THE MOON

LEGEND OF THE ANACONDA KING

CHRONICLES OF THE MOON

LEGEND OF THE ANACONDA KING

by Allan Frewin Jones

AN
APPLE
PAPERBACK

SCHOLASTIC INC

New York Toronto London Auckland Sydney
Mexico City New Delhi Hong Kong Buenos Aires

No part of this publication may be reproduced, stored in a retrieval system, or transmitted in any form or by any means, electronic, mechanical, photocopying, recording, or otherwise, without written permission of the publisher. For information regarding permission, write to Working Partners Limited, 1 Albion Place, London W6 0QT, United Kingdom.

ISBN 0-439-85670-1

Text copyright © 2006 by Working Partners Limited.
Created by Ben M. Baglio.
Cover illustrations copyright © 2006 by Ed Gazsi

All rights reserved. Published by Scholastic Inc., 557 Broadway, New York, NY 10012, by arrangement with Working Partners Limited. SCHOLASTIC, APPLE PAPERBACKS, and associated logos are trademarks and/or registered trademarks of Scholastic Inc.

12 11 10 9 8 7 6 5 4 3 2   6 7 8 9 10/0

Printed in the U.S.A.   40
First Scholastic printing, March 2006

PROLOGUE
The Amulet of Quilla

In 1538, the Spanish Conquistador Don Hernando Pizarro led an expeditionary force into the Inca heartlands to the south of Lake Titicaca. There he found vast wealth in silver and in gold, which he gathered and sent back across the Atlantic Ocean in great galley ships to the King of Spain. He learned from the native people that riches beyond the dreams of man were held in the sacred temples on the Island of the Sun and the Island of the Moon that lay in Lake Titicaca. Don Pizarro visited the islands, and his people claimed much treasure from them, but the greatest prize of all eluded him: the Amulet of Quilla, who was the Incan goddess of the moon.

Fearing that the amulet would be lost forever to the invading Spaniards, Coyata, the loyal handmaiden of Quilla, had secretly fled the island by night. She took the precious amulet to a hidden location in the rain forests of the Incan lands. For long, weary years the Spaniards searched for the amulet, but it was never found. . . .

Chapter One:
Incan Adventure

Olivia Christie looked up from the notebook she had been reading. Her father, an eminent professor of archaeology, had copied the history of the highly prized Amulet of Quilla from sixteenth-century documents he had discovered in the Spanish National Archaeological Museum in Madrid. In a few short days, he and his team would be in South America, taking up the ancient search for the sacred amulet of the Incan moon goddess.

And she would be with him. She could hardly wait.

~~~~~~

Olly swam slowly downward through the transparent waters of the vast lake, gazing out through her scuba mask in fascination and delight. Air was coming steadily to her through the oxygen regulator, but still her heart was pounding. She was taking her first open-water scuba dive after weeks of training back home in England, and it was very exciting.

At last she was putting all her practice and hard work into action.

She lifted her head. Above her she could see the waiting boat — a dark leaf shape on the surface of the lake, its outlines wavering in the endless, glittering, sunlit motion of the water. She looked down again into the depths — below her the water grew darker where the sunlight could not penetrate, and the lake floor was green and mysterious.

She was diving at a gentle slant, her body sheathed in an orange wet suit, broad fins strapped to her feet to help propel her through the water. Up above, the air was hot and dry, but underwater Olly felt pleasantly cool. She was hardly aware now of the weight of the oxygen tank strapped to her back. Her equipment had been thoroughly checked before the dive, and she felt perfectly safe — especially since she had two experienced divers along with her. She turned her head and saw her friend Josh Welles in his yellow wet suit, streams of bright bubbles rising up from his head, his legs working smoothly as he descended.

"Olly?" The voice was an electronic crackle in her ear. "How are you doing?"

She turned her head the other way, to look at Josh's twenty-two-year-old brother, Jonathan. He was the team leader; he had been scuba diving all

4

over the world. Twelve-year-old Josh had been diving for a couple of years, but Olly — two months older than Josh — had only learned to dive earlier that summer.

Olly gave the universal OK signal with her hand — finger and thumb together to form an *O*.

Shafts of shining blue light pierced the water, making her slow, careful dive down to the bottom of the lake seem like a magical journey through some mysterious other world.

She heard Josh's voice. "This is better than a swimming pool in Oxford, isn't it?" he said.

"It's fabulous," Olly agreed.

A couple of months ago, when the trip to the high Andes Mountains and a dive into Lake Titicaca had first been mentioned, Olly had not been very excited. She wasn't a great swimmer, and she had some uncomfortable memories of being underwater. When her father, Professor Kenneth Christie, had led an archaeological expedition to China earlier that summer, Olly had gone with him. But she had struggled trying to swim in an underground channel. There were no air pockets, and the distance had proven too long for Olly. If it hadn't been for Josh coming to her rescue, she might have drowned.

But Josh had encouraged her to learn to dive. "You can do it," he had told her. "In fact, you've *got* to do it, Olly. There might be ruined buildings under Lake Titicaca — ruins that are thousands and thousands of years old." Josh had looked at her solemnly. "You don't want to miss something as amazing as that, do you?"

Olly didn't, and so she had decided that she *would* learn to scuba dive. She was determined to see for herself whether there really were ancient ruins deep beneath the surface of the lake.

And now, just a few weeks and several intense scuba lessons later, she was diving confidently into unknown waters in Bolivia, and beginning another adventure in the ongoing quest to find all the fabled Talismans of the Moon.

Long, long ago, so the legend went, in different civilizations spread throughout the world, the priests and priestesses of the moon gods had called for the beautiful Talismans of the Moon to be made. Fashioned by expert craftsmen out of precious metals and priceless jewels, these talismans were said to hold an ancient and marvelous secret — a secret that would only be revealed when they were all brought together in the correct place.

Olly's father had discovered references to the legendary talismans in his studies of archaic writings. Gradually, he had begun to believe that the talismans were not simply the stuff of legends, but real artifacts that actually existed.

Since then, with his brilliant assistant Jonathan, Professor Christie had focused on discovering the talismans and unlocking their secret. Already, two had been found: one in the Valley of the Kings in Egypt, the other in the remote heartlands of China. Professor Christie now believed that clues which would lead him to a third Talisman of the Moon — the Amulet of Quilla — would be found amidst the ruins of Tiahuanaco. Jonathan had told Olly and Josh how to pronounce the city's name by breaking it down into syllables: "Tee-a-wah-na-co." This ancient city had originally been built on the shores of Lake Titicaca, but it was now stranded ten miles inland due to the gradual shrinking of the lake.

But there was an intriguing additional element to this expedition that Olly was excited to investigate and that had prompted her to learn to dive. Some archaeologists believed that there was a ruined city beneath the waters of Lake Titicaca — evidence of a society so old that, if real, its existence would completely change everything scientists believed about the origins of human civilization on Earth.

Olly knew that her father was skeptical about these extraordinary claims. As a scientist, he would require proof before he accepted that vast cities had existed in the world twenty thousand years earlier than anyone had previously thought. But Jonathan was fascinated by the theory.

"Olly! Josh! Can you see that dark ridge over to your left?" Jonathan's voice crackled in Olly's ear again, interrupting her thoughts. She turned her head. Jonathan was pointing toward the lake bottom. She swam toward him and peered down where he was indicating.

At first, all she could see was a formless mass of dark green in the water. Small, silver fish, striped with black, moved in swift shoals below her, skittering out of the way as she, Josh, and Jonathan slowly approached.

As Olly drew closer, she saw that beneath the thick vegetation and algae that covered the bottom of the lake, there appeared to be some solid shapes. Her eyes widened with astonishment as she realized she was looking at a great wall-like structure that stretched out across the lake bed.

"Wow!" she heard Josh exclaim in her ear. "Look at that!"

"I'm looking," Olly replied. But she could hardly believe her eyes. Being told by Jonathan that there might be a ruined city under the lake was one thing. Actually seeing signs of it in front of her eyes was something else.

As they swam together, only a few feet above the lake floor, more and more huge shapes began to emerge from the green gloom, half-covered in deep silt and dense vegetation.

Olly saw Jonathan unclip his camera from his belt and begin to take pictures.

"It is a city, isn't it?" Olly asked.

"It looks like one to me," Josh replied.

Olly heard Jonathan's voice. "Or it could be natural rock formations that look like ruined buildings," he said. "I really can't tell one way or the other at the moment."

"What do you mean?" Olly demanded. She pointed to where a sunken cleft stretched off into deeper waters like a long, straight road. "That has to be man-made!"

"But if this is a city," came the crackle of Josh's voice in her ear, "then it must have been built before there was ever a lake here. And the lake has been here since before the last ice age. That's thousands of years."

"And from what we know of human evolution," Jonathan's voice came in, "at that time our ancestors were wearing animal skins and living in caves, not building cities."

Pondering this information, Olly struck out strongly with her legs, gliding down between two green walls to follow the gulley. The bottom was flat between high sides.

"This has to be a road," she murmured. "What else could it possibly be?"

"I don't know," Jonathan's voice replied sharply in her ear. "But don't go too far. This is your first dive — I don't want you getting into trouble."

"I'll be fine," Olly replied. "I just want to see where this goes."

"By the look of it, it goes into much deeper water, Olly," Jonathan said. "Too deep for us."

"What we need is a bathyscaphe," Josh remarked. "One of those small submarine things that can go into really deep water. Then we could go right down to the very bottom. Olly — did you know that the lake is nearly nine hundred feet deep in some places?"

"No, I didn't," Olly said abstractedly, "I leave all that kind of stuff to you." She laughed. Her friend had a natural ability for collecting useless facts. She peered down the algae-covered valley along which she was swimming. The water was filled with bits of vegetation that drifted around her, making the water slightly murky.

"What do you mean by 'that kind of stuff'?" Josh questioned indignantly. "It's good to know something about the places we explore."

Olly looked up and around. She couldn't see Jonathan or Josh now. The high sides of the gulley enclosed her like a tunnel. If it wasn't for Josh's friendly voice in her ear, she would have found the experience rather eerie and disquieting. She could almost imagine that ancient eyes were peering out at her from among the rippling weeds.

She was certain the trench had been man-made. It seemed obvious to her that it was an ancient road. She pictured the people of a lost, drowned civilization, moving up and down this road thousands upon thousands of years ago, under a clear blue sky. She wondered how they had been able to build a city at a time when other humans were still learning how to make the simplest of stone tools.

"Did you know, for instance," came Josh's

voice again, "that the name *Titicaca* means 'rock of the puma'?"

"No, I didn't," Olly said, suddenly interested. "I like pumas. I like all big cats — but I think I like pumas best. Do they live around here?"

"What? In the lake?" Josh asked, sounding amused.

"No, in the Altiplano," Olly said, using the name given to this isolated region high in the Andes. "Oh!" she gasped suddenly. "What's that?" She had glimpsed a dark outline in the algae below her.

"What's what?" Josh asked.

"Just a second, I'm not sure," Olly replied. She swam downward until she was skimming the tall green fronds.

"Where are you, Olly?" came Jonathan's urgent voice. "You know you're supposed to stay within sight of me."

"I'm fine," Olly said. "I'm just following the road."

"Well, come out of there so I can see you," Jonathan ordered. "Don't start getting adventurous; you could wind up in trouble."

"OK," Olly promised. "Just a minute."

The tall waterweeds swayed around her as she cut through them. She had almost reached the dark object now.

She gave a gasp of shock, and bit back a scream as the weeds parted to reveal eyes! Something was watching her through the quivering weeds. She hesitated, and an undercurrent drew the curtain of green farther aside so that, for a fleeting moment, Olly clearly saw the face that stared at her.

It was the exquisitely carved face of a cat.

Chapter Two: ∾
The Island of the Moon

Olly broke the surface and swam toward the waiting boat, the curious artifact with the cat's face on it tucked into her belt. A hand reached down and helped her climb the short ladder into the vessel. The boat belonged to a local man named Carlos. He smiled down at her as she clambered awkwardly out of the lake. He had the dark skin, broad cheekbones, and jet black hair of the native Aymara Indians.

Olly unstrapped the heavy oxygen tank and Carlos slipped it off her back. Then Olly collapsed in the stern of the boat, catching her breath. "Look what I found!" she said after a moment, holding the artifact out to Carlos.

It was about the size of her hand, thin, curved, and carved into the shape of a cat's face with wide, staring eyes. It was green-tinged and felt a little slimy from being so long under the waters of the lake.

"It is a puma," Carlos said.

Olly's eyes widened. "Really?" she breathed,

surprised that she and Josh had been talking about pumas only seconds before she found the thing.

A splashing sound drew Carlos to the edge of the boat, and a few moments later Josh climbed aboard, followed closely by Jonathan.

"What have you got there?" Jonathan asked.

"It's a puma," Olly told him proudly.

Jonathan sat down beside her. "So it is," he said, gently lifting it out of her hands. He turned it over. "Very nice."

Olly frowned. "Is that all you can say?" she responded. "I bring up a priceless archaeological find from the bottom of the lake and all you can say is '*very nice*'?"

Jonathan laughed. "I'm sorry, Olly," he said. "But lots of these things have been found. It's made of pottery and was probably part of a chalice of worship or an incense burner."

"How old is it?" Josh asked, peering over his brother's shoulder.

"It looks like it predates the Incas," Jonathan said. "It could be anything from eight hundred to fifteen hundred years old — maybe even older. It's a lovely find, Olly — but it's not all that unusual."

"Does that mean that I can keep it?" Olly asked eagerly.

"Sorry," Jonathan said. "It'll have to go to a museum. But I don't see why we can't ask them to include a little display card with 'Found by Olivia Christie' on it."

Olly liked the sound of that.

Jonathan looked from Olly to Josh. "So, are you two worn out yet, or would you like to see the ruins now?"

"I'm not worn out at all," Olly said. "Let's go!"

Jonathan warned them that with the thin air at this high altitude, they would tire more quickly. Olly had felt a little breathless at times, but she was determined not to let it stop her — especially when there was something interesting to explore.

Lake Titicaca lay in a lofty valley of the Altiplano — the Bolivian high plane — which rose almost twelve thousand feet above sea level. All around the plateau, snowcapped mountains soared to over seventeen thousand feet. Up here the air was clear and thin, and all activity was an effort.

Jonathan asked Carlos to take them to the Island of the Moon. As the motorboat sped along, Olly and Josh struggled out of their wet suits. By the time the boat reached the island, they were all toweled down and changed into T-shirts and shorts.

The group waved to Carlos, then jumped into

the shallow, crystal clear water and waded up onto dry land. The island reared sharply out of the lake and required a steep climb to get up off the beach. The sun-bleached rocks were broken up by patches of pale, wiry grass and scrubby bushes.

Olly would never have admitted it, but she found the climb difficult — the thin air was catching up with her, and the midday sun beat down on them relentlessly. But at last, they stood on the highest point of the island. Olly ran an arm across her sweating forehead, and paused to get her breath back. It was some comfort to her to see that Jonathan and Josh were also panting.

Behind them, she could see the mainland stretching away into the distance, some twenty miles from the island. In the other direction, she could see the long, dark ridge of the much larger Island of the Sun, and beyond that — gray-blue in the haze — the farther shores of Lake Titicaca.

Once they had recovered, Jonathan led the way along the high back of the island and down a rough slope. He pointed. "Welcome to Inak Uyu," he said. On a broad, terraced plateau, halfway down the slope, Olly saw the remains of thick stone walls jutting from the surrounding undergrowth.

"These are the remains of an Incan Moon

Temple," Jonathan explained, as they made their way down to the plateau. "It dates back about eight hundred years — but it was built on an already-existing site. Recent findings have proved that people have lived on this island for at least four thousand years."

"I read that, too," Josh added. "The pre-Inca people are known as the *Tiwanaku*. And before them were the Pucara people, and before that —"

"Did you know that the Moon Temple was staffed entirely by women?" Olly interrupted, eyeing Josh with amusement. Sometimes he acted like he was the only one who knew anything! "They were called the *Mamacona* — the Chosen Women. Men weren't allowed here at all, except to make sacrifices to the moon goddess, Quilla."

Josh grinned. "You've been doing some research," he said.

"I have," she responded. "You're not the only one who can read."

Jonathan laughed at their lighthearted rivalry. "Come on," he said, "let's explore."

Olly hadn't realized just how massive the ancient stone walls were until she was in among them. The perfectly shaped blocks of masonry reared high above her head.

The main part of the temple consisted of three long, broken walls around what had once been a large courtyard. The walls were punctuated by several curious doorways that seemed to lead nowhere.

"What are these for?" Olly asked, standing under one of the great square entrances. It was as if, for some reason, the ancient architects had set four doorways inside one another, each one a little smaller than the one before it. The final, smallest doorway was blocked by a flat wall of stones.

"They're called niches," Jonathan explained. "We haven't really worked out their role in Incan rituals, but we've seen them in several different locations. We think they may have been special places where the high priestess sat during important ceremonies."

They walked through the ruins while Jonathan explained how, for millennia, pilgrims would have come from all over the region to worship at the Temple of the Moon and the Temple of the Sun, and make sacrifices to their gods.

"Sometimes it was something as simple as a handful of corn offered up to please the sun god," Josh told them. "Or woven clothes might be burned in a sacrificial fire. But sometimes animals were killed. It was very important to keep the gods happy."

They spent an hour or so in the ruins before heading back to Carlos and the boat. They set off under a clear, blue sky. Olly leaned over the side, letting the sun-dappled water run through her fingers as they headed for the mainland.

"Carlos?" she called. "Can't you go a bit faster?"

Carlos grinned at her. "Sí, señorita, I go very fast for you."

He was true to his word. The boat took a leap forward, cleaving the water as it scudded across the lake, leaving a broad white wake of foam behind them.

Olly let out a yell of delight, her long dark hair floating in the wind, the air whipping past her face and ripping at her clothes. "That's more like it!"

Josh was grinning, too, as the wind caught his shaggy blond hair and dragged it across his face. "Go for it, Carlos!" he called. "As fast as you can!"

"No, no," Jonathan groaned. "No faster, please."

Olly looked at him. He was clinging grimly to the back of the boat, and looking rather green.

"But this is fun!" she shouted above the high-pitched roar of the motor. The boat clipped a wave, rising and falling as the spray splashed Olly's face. "Whooo!" she gasped, hanging on tight. "See what I mean?"

Jonathan seemed to go a slightly deeper shade of green.

"Some people just don't know how to enjoy themselves!" Olly yelled heartlessly as the small motorboat sped across the brilliant blue waters under the blazing afternoon sun.

~~~~

Olly had been accompanying her father on his continent-hopping archaeological adventures ever since her mother had died in an airplane crash in New Guinea two years ago. On these trips, Olly's grandmother, Audrey Beckmann, kept an eye on Olly and her father, making sure they ate properly and had clean clothes to wear. She was an intelligent and determined woman — and a qualified teacher — who acted as tutor for both Olly and Josh.

Jonathan and Josh's mother, Natasha Welles, was an internationally famous movie star. She was always having to travel to different locations for filming, so Mrs. Beckmann had suggested that Josh accompany his brother and the Christies on their expeditions. Josh and Olly were best friends, so the arrangement worked very well.

Olly loved this exciting, freewheeling life, although, in her opinion, her grandma was a little too insistent on keeping up the schoolwork, while she and Josh would much rather spend time exploring. Even the fact that the two friends had been directly involved in finding the first two Talismans of the Moon didn't hold any sway with Audrey Beckmann, and all Olly's persuasiveness was wasted once her grandmother had made up her mind. Olly and Josh loaded their scuba gear into their Land Rover, and then Jonathan drove them the fifteen miles to the small town where they were staying. As they sped along the arid dirt road, the starkly beautiful landscape of the Andes spread out around them, — the sunburned rock and rough pastureland were dotted with grazing llamas and alpacas. Far away, they could see snowcapped mountain peaks. Even in the high-noon sun the view of the icy High Sierras gave Olly a chill.

They were staying in a beautiful house owned by a friend of Josh's mother, a retired actress named Jazmine Romero. It had white, adobe walls and a roof of curved terra-cotta tiles. Josh and Olly had adjoining second-floor rooms, with a shared balcony from which they could look out over the picturesque buildings of the town and watch the comings and goings of the local Aymara Indians.

The group arrived at the house to find Olly's father already there. While they had been scuba diving in Lake Titicaca, Professor Christie had set off to explore the ruins of the ancient ceremonial site of Tiahuanaco.

Usually, the professor's expeditions included field archaeologists, experts, and local diggers, but this trip was on a much smaller scale. He had to be back in England in two weeks to attend an important international seminar. There simply wasn't time for a full excavation — but his recent research in Madrid had convinced him that even a brief trip to Bolivia might yield some useful clues as to the whereabouts of the long-lost Amulet of Quilla.

The professor and Olly's grandmother were sitting at a table under the wide veranda of the house, drinking fresh juice from tall, chilled glasses. Mrs. Beckmann was reading a newspaper, elegantly dressed as always in a cream silk blouse and khaki linen trousers. Olly's father sat opposite her, his gray hair a wild thatch, his clothes rumpled and dusty. He was totally absorbed in the papers he was reading.

Typical Dad! Olly thought fondly. Completely lost in his own academic world, the professor was unaware of his unkempt appearance.

Mrs. Beckmann looked up. "Did you enjoy your swim?" she asked.

"We had a great time," Olly replied. "I found this." She placed the pottery puma face delicately into her grandma's hands. "It's going to be displayed in a museum. There'll be a note next to it with my name on it."

"Well, that's lovely," her grandmother said with a smile. "It's a cat!"

"It's a puma, actually," Olly said, throwing herself down in a chair and reaching for the jug of juice that stood on the table with a couple of empty glasses. "How about you, Dad? Find anything amazing?"

There was no response from her father.

"Earth to Dad!" Olly called in a much louder voice. "Come in, Dad!"

Professor Christie peered absentmindedly at her through his half-moon spectacles. "Oh, hello there," he said vaguely.

Now that she had his attention, Olly asked her question again.

Her father frowned. "It's been good and bad," he told her.

Jonathan and Josh joined them at the table. The

ice clinked as Olly poured them each a tall glass of juice.

The professor glanced at Jonathan. "I was able to see the Puma Punku Stone — the engraved slab that Pizarro mentioned in his letters to the King of Spain."

"That's great news!" Jonathan exclaimed, leaning forward excitedly. "And did the markings match what Pizarro had claimed?"

"Yes," the professor confirmed. "The designs engraved on the stone do seem to be a coded depiction of the handmaiden Coyata's journey from the Temple of the Moon as she escaped with the Amulet of Quilla. But as Pizarro said in his letters — the stone is incomplete." He frowned. "I spoke with the curator of the site, and he told me that over the years a great many people have searched the area for the missing part of the Puma Punku Stone."

Olly looked at him. "So, what do we know so far about the Amulet of Quilla?" she asked, sitting back and stretching out her legs.

"We know that Coyata took it from the temple on the Island of the Moon to keep it out of the hands of the Spanish Conquistadors," her father began. "She first took it to Tiahuanaco, but Coyata knew it wouldn't be safe there for very long. So she waited in hiding for a moonless night, and then she journeyed to a forested area by a great river." The frustration showed in his voice. "But we have no idea in which direction she traveled to reach this forested area, or how far she journeyed."

Olly frowned. "A river that runs through a forest, huh?" she said. "Well, it's a start."

Jonathan shook his head. "Bolivia is a big country, Olly, and it's full of rivers," he told her. "Most of them pass through rain forests at some stage. You could search for a lifetime and not even come close to finding the place where the amulet was taken."

"Then the answer's pretty obvious," Olly said firmly. "We have to find the missing piece of the stone so we can read the rest of Coyata's story." She nodded thoughtfully, and fixed her father with a stern gaze. "You'll need some sharp-eyed people on this mission," she said. "Here's an idea: Josh and I will go with you to Tiahuanaco in the morning, and we won't give up looking till we find it!" She lifted her eyebrows. "What do you say?"

"It's a tempting offer, Olly," her father said with a smile. "But I don't think it's going to be lying around anywhere obvious. Pizarro's men realized the significance of the Puma Punku Stone — and they searched very thoroughly for the missing piece. My worry is that the stone didn't originate in the city of Tiahuanaco at all, but was brought there at some later date. The missing section could have been left behind or lost on the journey."

"You could be wrong," Olly pointed out hopefully.

"Yes, I could," her father admitted. "Which is why I've invited a local expert to come and examine the site with me." He turned to Jonathan. "Doctor Vargas is coming up from La Paz tomorrow morning. I'm hoping he will be able to shed some light on the problem."

"Then you two will definitely be staying with me," Mrs. Beckmann put in, eyeing Olly and Josh. "The last thing your father will need is the two of you racing around getting in everyone's way. Besides, you have lessons in the morning — you know that."

"But we could help," Olly urged. "Studying can wait, just this once, can't they?"

Mrs. Beckmann arched an eyebrow. "If I had a dollar for every time you've said that, Olivia, I'd be a rich woman," she said. Olly opened her mouth to speak again, but her grandma lifted a silencing hand. "Besides," she went on. "I have something rather interesting planned for the two of you tomorrow."

"Oh, OK," Olly replied. That didn't sound so bad.

"What is it?" Josh asked.

"We're going to the market," Mrs. Beckmann told him, "where you're going to get a chance to watch the local weavers at work. I'm told it's quite fascinating."

Olly and Josh looked at each other in disbelief. Olly had very serious doubts about how fascinating weaving could be.

Chapter Three: ∼
Legends and Looms

"Do you know what's really exciting about weaving?" Olly asked Josh the following morning as the two friends sat on the veranda steps, waiting for her grandma.

Josh looked at her in surprise. "No, what?"

"Absolutely nothing!" Olly declared.

Josh laughed. "It won't be that bad," he said. He was happy that today's lessons involved a trip outside. It could have been worse: It was a gloriously sunny morning and they might otherwise have been stuck indoors struggling with math or geography.

Josh and Olly were both wearing hats to shield them from the fierce sun. The air quickly heated up once the sun climbed above the mountain peaks, but at night, under a clear sky shining with frosty stars, temperatures plummeted dramatically. The Altiplano was a place of extremes, where you could sunbathe at noon and freeze to death overnight.

Jazmine's house stood on high ground overlooking the town. Directly below, simple, rustic buildings jostled for space, while farther down the hill the buildings were larger and more ornate. Josh could see that the broad marketplace in the middle of the town was already filling with people.

"Is everyone ready?" Audrey Beckmann asked, arriving on the veranda.

Josh and Olly got up and followed her down into the town. The place was full of activity, and they were quickly caught up in the hustle and bustle of the crowd.

The local Aymara women wore bulky, brightly colored skirts and woolen shawls. The men were dressed in colorful ponchos and wore close-fitting, pointed, woolen caps. Olly and Josh noticed that some of the women carried babies in woven slings across their backs.

The broad marketplace was packed with produce. There were a few large stalls, but many of the merchants simply occupied a space on the ground, their wares spread out in heaps on thick straw mats. Josh saw a huge variety of things for sale, from corn on the cob, haba beans, watermelons, and tomatoes to balls of colored yarn, metal pots and pans, and woven fabrics. Children ran in and out of people's legs, laughing and calling to one another. Meanwhile, the delicious smells of soups and stews drifted through the air from outdoor kitchens, making Josh feel hungry even though it hadn't been long since he'd had breakfast.

As he gazed around, Josh noticed a man who seemed, for a moment, to be standing watching them. He wasn't an Indian — he was dressed in a white linen suit that showed off his golden tan, and he had white hair that was swept back from a high forehead. But an instant later, he was lost in the crowd, and Josh was distracted by the calls of the market sellers.

They made their way slowly across the busy market, following Olly's grandma, who threaded a path through the crowds. Josh felt quite relieved when they finally emerged from the riotous marketplace and entered a less hectic area of small workshops and enclosed stalls.

"This way," Mrs. Beckmann said, leading them into an adobe building. The large, open room was piled high with fabrics woven in a seemingly endless variety of colorful patterns. The walls were hung with more lengths of material, a little like flags — although Josh had never seen flags with such amazingly intricate designs on them.

A woman wearing a traditional pollera skirt and a white blouse came to greet them. Josh guessed that she was in her forties, and took an instant liking to her round, smiling face and bright eyes.

"You must be Olly and Josh," the woman said, smiling at the two friends. "I have heard all about you. My name is Fabiola." She looked at Olly's grandma. "Audrey says you wish to learn how to weave?"

Olly opened her mouth to speak, but Josh stopped her just in time with a discreet poke in the ribs. It would be just like Olly to say something embarrassing about what she really thought of weaving.

Fabiola shepherded them across the room. "Come, come, I will show you."

"I'll leave them with you for the time being, Fabiola, if that's all right," said Olly's grandmother. "I have a few things to buy in the market." She turned to Olly and Josh. "I won't be long," she said. "You can tell me all about it when I get back."

"Are you enjoying your visit to our country, Olly?" Fabiola asked.

"It's absolutely wonderful," Olly replied enthusiastically, as she followed Fabiola toward a doorway into a wide courtyard, where rows of women sat on mats on the ground, working at small, horizontal, handheld looms.

"Here we weave mantras," Fabiola explained. "A

mantra is one of the most prized possessions of an Aymara family. It is useful as well as decorative. It can be slung across the shoulders and used to carry things."

"I saw that in the market," Josh said. "There were women carrying babies in them."

Fabiola nodded. "Babies or firewood or vegetables — a mantra can be used for everything. They are also spread on the ground and used as mats, and as you can see, they make wonderful wall hangings." She pointed to one of the flag-shaped mantras that hung above the doorway. "Each town has its own designs," she explained. "The patterns are passed down through generations — many go back hundreds and hundreds of years."

Josh gazed up at the mantra over the door. It had a complex inner design of red, black, and yellow symbols, and a border of green and blue squares, many of which contained squat, stylized figures with their arms held in various positions.

"That mantra was woven by my great-grandmother," Fabiola told him. "It is a very ancient design." She looked at the friends, her eyes twinkling. "Would you like to try some weaving yourselves?"

"We'll probably make a mess of it," Olly said.

But Fabiola simply laughed and led them over to a couple of spare looms in one corner of the courtyard. "These are backstrap looms," she told them. "Aymara women have been using them for a thousand years or more."

Josh looked at the simple looms in fascination. Around the courtyard, each woman sat with her legs stretched out in front of her. The far end of the loom's framework was attached, by a cord, to a peg set in the ground about a half yard beyond her bare feet. The other end was held firm by a belt fastened around the woman's waist. There was a steady click and thud as the weavers worked.

Fabiola called an elderly woman over to help, and Olly and Josh were soon strapped into their own looms. Fabiola sat at Josh's side. The other woman, Beatriz, helped Olly.

Both looms already held a half-finished length of cloth. "Mantras are made in two halves," Fabiola explained to Josh. "Each half is woven separately, and then the mantra is stitched together. On the loom, the long threads are called the warp, the crosswise threads are the weft." She leaned across him, her long, brown fingers moving nimbly as she showed him how to weave the threads.

Josh watched carefully, bewildered at first by the speed at which Fabiola was working. But gradually, as the minutes passed, he began to grasp the rhythm and pattern of it. "Could I do a bit of the design you showed us on that mantra above the door?" he asked. "The one with those funny men on it." He liked the little stumpy figures with their arms going in different directions — it kind of reminded him of a football referee, almost as if the different positions might mean something.

Fabiola nodded and watched carefully as Josh made his first clumsy attempt at weaving. It was demanding work, but Fabiola was encouraging and patient, and slowly Josh began to get the hang of it.

He heard Olly laugh. "I'm hopeless at this!" she sighed. "My fingers are all thumbs. How are you doing, Josh?"

Josh didn't look up or reply. He was too busy concentrating on his work.

"He is doing very well," Fabiola said. "He has a real feel for it."

"Really?" Olly said. "Good for him. Weave me a mantra, Josh."

"Sshh!" he hissed at her. "I'm going to lose my place if you keep chattering."

"I'm sorry, Beatriz," Olly said. "I'm obviously not cut out to be a weaver. Is it OK if I just sit and watch Josh?" She shuffled over and sat cross-legged beside her friend.

"Keep quiet, OK?" Josh told her.

"Of course," Olly muttered, sounding slightly miffed.

But it wasn't in Olly's nature to sit in silence for any length of time. "I found a piece of pottery on the bottom of Lake Titicaca when we went scuba diving yesterday," Olly told the two women. "It had a puma's face on it."

"The puma was always a divine animal to the Aymara people," Beatriz remarked wisely, in her cracked old voice. "Many people still believe that eclipses are caused by a sacred puma biting pieces out of the sun and the moon. There are not so many pumas in these parts nowadays because there are so many people. But the pumas live on in legends."

"I'd like to know more about the history of Bolivia," Olly said. "About the Incas and the conquistadors. The Incas had a really powerful empire at one time, didn't they? But then the conquistadors invaded."

"That was because of the wickedness of Atahualpa," Beatriz said. "He stole the kingship from his brother, Wascar, and imprisoned him. In doing so, Atahualpa brought down a curse upon his family. He had broken the true and sacred line of the Inca kings, and as a punishment, the gods sent the Spanish Conquistadors to destroy the empire and bring five hundred years of darkness to the land."

Josh glanced at Olly, noticing the fascination on her face. She knew all about families and curses — in fact, her own family was supposed to be cursed! It all had to do with a sacred scroll that had been taken from an ancient Egyptian tomb over one hundred years ago. According to the writings on the scroll, unless it was replaced, the first born son in each generation of the Christie family would die a premature death. And the creepy thing was that people *had* died. In fact, a great-uncle of Olly's had been killed in a shipwreck while trying to take the scroll back to Egypt and return it to the tomb.

"The conquistadors arrived here in the sixteenth century," Olly said, interrupting Josh's thoughts, "so I suppose the five hundred years of darkness are almost up."

"That is true," Beatriz agreed, nodding. "It is said that when the Amulet of Quilla is found, the darkness will be lifted."

Josh looked up in surprise, his weaving temporarily forgotten. "We're here to try and find the Amulet of Quilla!" he explained.

"Then may good fortune go with you on your quest," Beatriz declared solemnly.

"I don't suppose you know any legends that say *where* the amulet was hidden, do you?" Olly asked.

Beatriz began to speak in a soft, low voice, her eyes great pools of blackness very deep and dark as she looked from Josh to Olly. Josh's hands fell still and he watched her intently, hardly remembering to breathe as he listened to the strange tale.

"It is said that Quilla's handmaiden, the beautiful and virtuous Coyata, was guided on her journey by a sacred puma," Beatriz intoned. "It was the puma who told her to leave the Temple of the Moon and then Tiahuanaco, and seek refuge in the forest. After several days of traveling, they came to a deep valley with high walls of rock that could not be climbed by man or beast. Their way forward was blocked by a curtain of fire that filled the valley from side to side. Coyata despaired of getting through, and she was about to turn back when the puma walked into the flames and vanished from her sight. Coyata's faith in her guide was so strong that she followed him into the flames and walked — unharmed — to the other side. Beyond the wall of fire, she found the puma waiting for her beside a temple, hidden among the trees. Within its walls, she placed the Amulet of Quilla. And there it has remained, undiscovered, for all these long, dark years."

"Does the legend say exactly where all this took place?" Olly asked, her voice a breathless whisper.

There was a moment of silence. And then the old lady nodded and smiled.

Josh's eyes widened. "You know where Coyata hid the amulet?" he breathed.

"Yes," Beatriz said. "It is in a very secret place."

Josh could hardly believe his ears. Did the old lady really know where the Amulet of Quilla was hidden? Had the answer been part of an old legend all along?

"But *where*?" Olly asked, her voice cracking with excitement.

Beatriz smiled a secretive smile and leaned forward to whisper. "The legend says it is in the Lair of the Anaconda King!"

Chapter Four:
Worrying News

"The Lair of the Anaconda King," Olly murmured. To her, it seemed like the whole world held its breath in the few moments following Beatriz's astounding announcement.

Josh stared at the old woman. Wrinkles mapped her face, but her skin shined like polished wood, and her deep black eyes sparkled like distant stars. A profound silence pressed against Josh's ears, making his head ring. Olly, too, was gazing at Beatriz with her mouth open, frozen in amazement.

And then Beatriz laughed and the spell was broken. Reality came rushing back. Josh heard again the clack and rattle of the weaving, and the everyday sounds of the nearby marketplace.

"And where is the Lair of the Anaconda King?" Olly asked.

Beatriz laughed again and shook her head, lifting her hand to shake a finger at Olly. "No, no," she said. "I do not give away the secret." She put a finger to her lips, still shaking her head.

"Beatriz, *please*," Olly begged.

Fabiola's face broke into a wide smile. "She is teasing you, Olly," she said. "No one knows where the Lair of the Anaconda King is." She spread her hands. "It is just a legend. Maybe it does not even exist. You want my opinion? If there ever was such a thing as the Amulet of Quilla, then the conquistadors took it long ago. It's gone forever."

"No," Josh put in. "I don't think that's true. Olly's father has seen letters from Hernando Pizarro to the Spanish king. Pizarro spent years searching for the amulet — but he never found it."

"Or maybe Olly's father has not yet found the letter in which Don Pizarro tells the king that he *did* find it," Fabiola pointed out.

Josh looked at her uneasily — that was a disturbing thought. And it was quite possible, too. If that one vital document was simply missing from the five-hundred-year-old archives, it would change everything. The Amulet of Quilla could have been found and sent back to Spain, then melted down to fill the gold vaults of the insatiable conquistadors. After all, thousands of other Incan artifacts had met a similar fate.

Beatriz frowned at Fabiola and said something to her in the Aymara language.

Fabiola smiled and shrugged. "Beatriz says I have no faith. She says the amulet is still hidden in the forest and that one day it will be found. Maybe she is right."

"I hope she is," Olly said fervently. "Otherwise we might as well pack our bags and go home."

~~~~~

It was early evening, and Olly and Josh were setting the table on the veranda of Jazmine's house. They were going to eat dinner outdoors. The sun was just sinking behind the mountains, and cool shadows were spilling across the valley. It was still pleasant under the clear, pale sky, and heaters lined the veranda to ward off the oncoming chill of night. Lanterns, hanging from the roof, gave out a warm yellow glow, and mouthwatering cooking smells drifted from the kitchen where Jazmine's cook was preparing the evening meal.

Olly had discovered — by poking around in the kitchen — that they were going to be eating chicken and rice, accompanied by *oca* and other local vegetables. The cuts of chicken were bubbling gently in a homemade, spicy sauce called *llajhua*, while the cook shredded lettuce for an accompanying salad.

The growl of an approaching car caught the attention of the two friends.

"It's Jonathan and your dad," Josh said, leaning over the veranda and waving as the Land Rover came rumbling up the dirt road. "I hope they've had a good day."

Olly peered down at the vehicle as it came to a halt. She thought that the expressions on the faces of the two men did not look hopeful as they climbed out. They were talking animatedly as they came up the steps to the veranda.

"I'm sorry, Jonathan," the professor was saying. "But those pictures you took of the formations on the lake bottom don't convince me that there was a civilization in these parts twenty thousand years earlier than is currently believed. Analysis of core samples of the soil has proved that the size of the lake is constantly changing. If those lumps and bumps are the remains of a city, then it must have been built when the lake was much smaller than it is today."

"I agree," Jonathan argued. "But it's thought that Lake Titicaca has been shrinking for the last four thousand years. So if they are buildings, when could the city have been built? Surely, it must have been well before the first people were thought to have arrived here."

Professor Christie shook his head. "Not

necessarily," he said. "The earliest finds show human occupation in this area as far back as six thousand years ago. A catastrophic landslip or earthquake could have inundated a shoreline city at any time over that period. I need far more evidence before I'm going to believe that everything we understand about the evolution of human civilization is wrong!"

"But if it's true," Jonathan urged, "then the talismans themselves could be thousands of years older than we currently think they are."

Professor Christie smiled and rested his hand on his excited young assistant's shoulder. "It is possible. And perhaps the truth will come to light when all the talismans are brought together," he said. "In the meantime, let's not get sidetracked by unproven theories."

Olly greeted them at the top of the steps. "Hello, you two," she said. "How did it go?"

"Doctor Vargas wasn't able to help us very much, I'm afraid," her father replied. "He agreed that the Puma Punku Stone tells the legend of Coyata's flight from the Temple of the Moon, but beyond that, he knew no more than we do."

"And I don't suppose you happened to trip over the missing piece of the stone tablet?" Olly asked.

"No such luck," Jonathan said gloomily. He sniffed, his face brightening a little. "That smells good," he added.

"It'll be ready in a few minutes," Olly's grandma told him as she stepped out onto the veranda. "By the time you two have washed the grime off and changed out of those grubby clothes, it'll be on the table."

Olly linked her arm through her father's, looking up into his weary, disheartened face. "Don't worry, Dad," she said optimistically. "The five hundred years of darkness are almost up. You'll find the Lair of the Anaconda King. I know you will."

Her father stared at her. "What are you talking about, Olivia?" he asked.

Olly grinned. "I'll tell you all about it over dinner," she said. "You may have had a boring day, but Josh and I have learned some really interesting stuff." Her eyes shined. "Stuff that just might help us make the legends come true. . . ."

~~~~~

Later that evening, Josh was in his room, typing out an e-mail on the laptop he had borrowed from his brother. He yawned. It was nearly bedtime, but first he wanted to write to his mother.

From downstairs drifted the sound of Jazmine

playing a guitar and singing a local song, the melody as haunting and beautiful as the Altiplano landscape itself. Through the window, the lights of the town were a friendly glow in the wide darkness. And above the dark mountain peaks a million stars seemed to shine in the sky, shining more brightly than Josh had ever seen before. It was at night that he really got the feeling they were living on the roof of the world — as the Altiplano was sometimes known — and that the stars were almost within reach.

There was a knock on his door, and Olly burst in without waiting for a response. She was in her pajamas.

Josh gave her an inquiring look.

"I just want to borrow that Aymara phrasebook of yours," she said. "I'd like to be able to say a bit more than 'yes,' 'no,' and 'hello' before we leave."

"It's by the bed," Josh told her.

She climbed across his bed and retrieved the book from a small table. "What are you doing?" she asked, sitting down and flicking idly through the pages.

"I'm writing to my mom," Josh told her. "I'm telling her what we've been up to so far." He glanced over his shoulder at Olly. "She likes to be kept up to date."

"And what's *she* doing?" Olly asked. "Is she still hacking her way through the Australian bush with our old friend, Ethan Cain?"

"Yes, as far as I know," Josh replied.

Ethan Cain was his mother's rich, American computer-genius boyfriend. On the surface, he seemed charming and friendly — an open, trustworthy man with a harmless amateur interest in archaeology. But Josh and Olly knew better. Under the pleasant facade, Cain was ruthless and treacherous — and he wanted the Talismans of the Moon for himself. Twice now, the two friends had thwarted Ethan's underhanded attempts to reach the talismans before Professor Christie's team found them. In both cases — in Egypt and in China — it was only Olly and Josh's quick thinking that had stopped Ethan.

But the real problem for the two friends was that no one believed Ethan Cain was a criminal. He had smiled and lied his way out of trouble very smoothly, and they had actually been reprimanded for making accusations against him. It was particularly upsetting for Josh to know that his mother was dating a lying, cheating creep like Cain, but to be unable to prove it.

Olly and Josh had been very relieved when they had learned that Natasha Welles and Ethan Cain were on an adventure holiday on the far side of the world. The last Josh had heard from his mother, she and Cain were camped near Ayers Rock. She had even sent a few digital photographs, showing the two of them standing with their backs to the rock, looking cool and glamorous, like a celebrity couple from a glossy magazine.

"The farther away Ethan Cain is, the better I like it," Olly announced. "Oh — say hi to your mom from me."

Josh added a few final words to his e-mail and then pressed send. He grinned at Olly as the e-mail vanished. "I've told her we're hot on the trail of the amulet," he said. "That should drive Ethan wild!"

∿∿∿

As soon as Josh woke up the following morning, he opened up the laptop to check for a reply from his mother.

He sat up in bed with the computer on his knees, yawning as he checked his e-mail. There was one new message. He smiled — it was from his mother. But his smile faded as he read her brief note.

Dearest Jonathan and Josh,
I'm feeling a little disappointed right now — Ethan's just had some bad news from California and he's had to

rush off to catch a plane home! Apparently, there's some big problem at the office that he has got to deal with in person. Typical, isn't it? Still, we only had four days of our vacation left, so it's not a total disaster. I'm going to take the opportunity to spend the rest of my time here sunbathing — you know how much Ethan hates that!

Anyway, that's all for now. I'm off to Alice Springs in the morning. I'll bring you home a didjeridoo if I can fit one in my luggage.

Love to everyone,
Mom

Josh frowned. Only a few hours after he had sent an e-mail telling his mother that they were on the trail of the amulet, Ethan had suddenly had to leave Australia. Josh had a nasty feeling that the two things might be connected.

Grabbing the laptop, he leaped out of bed and raced into Olly's room. "Olly! Wake up!" he said, shaking her violently.

Olly let out a wordless shout and struggled into a sitting position, rubbing her eyes. "What are you doing?" she growled when she noticed who had woken her.

Josh knew that Olly wasn't at her best in the early morning — but the bad news from Australia couldn't wait. He set the computer on her lap. "Read that!" he said.

Olly glared at him for a moment, then turned her head to read Natasha's e-mail.

There was a short pause. Olly's eyes narrowed as she read the e-mail through a second time. She looked at Josh. "I don't like the sound of that," she declared, echoing his own thoughts. "Do *you* think it's true?" she added. "About him having to deal with a work problem?"

"It might be," Josh began dubiously. "But I think it was a mistake to mention the amulet in that e-mail I sent last night."

Olly nodded.

"I think Ethan probably made up that story about work as an excuse to leave Australia," Josh went on darkly. "I reckon he's been waiting to find out how we were getting along — and now he's going to sneak over here and try to find the Amulet of Quilla before we do."

Chapter Five:
The Puma Punku Stone

Following their morning lessons, Olly and Josh were out on the veranda finishing their lunch, when Jonathan came roaring up the dirt road in the Land Rover. He and the professor had driven down to Tiahuanaco after breakfast; they weren't expected back for several hours yet. Jonathan brought the vehicle to a halt and came running up the steps.

Olly stared at him. "What are you doing back so early?" she called.

"I forgot the GPS," he said, disappearing into the house.

Olly knew what he meant. The GPS was a handheld, computerized device that used satellite technology to give pinpoint accuracy when recording the position of anything — from a single rock to a whole city.

She nudged Josh. "This is our chance to see the ruins," she hissed. "We can go back to Tiahuanaco with him."

It was only a couple of minutes before Jonathan reappeared and Olly was able to make her suggestion.

"Why not?" he said, climbing back into the Land Rover. "All aboard."

Olly didn't need telling twice. She quickly gulped the rest of her lunch and ran inside to tell her grandma where they were going. Then she and Josh piled into the Land Rover.

It was a seventy-mile drive to the ancient ruins, traveling a dusty, bumpy road that cut sharply through rolling hills. To their right, when they got a good view, they could see the sparkling blue waters of Lake Titicaca.

"Rats!" Josh said suddenly. "I should have brought my camera." His mother had given him a new digital camera, but he had left it sitting on his bedside table back at Jazmine's house.

"Don't worry about it," Jonathan told him. "We've taken plenty of pictures."

Olly was feeling slightly queasy. Rushing the end of her lunch seemed to have given her indigestion. But it wasn't too bad, and she decided not to mention it to Jonathan. She didn't want him to tease her, the way she had teased him in the motorboat — or worse, insist on taking her home before she'd seen the ruins!

As they approached the outskirts of the Tiahuanaco ruins, Olly fought her indigestion and stared out the window. Huge, shaped slabs of glossy, dark-gray stone lay half-buried in the ground.

"Those stones are basalt," Jonathan said. "Some of them weigh over four hundred thousand pounds. We don't really know why they're here. They could be collapsed buildings, or they might be stones that were abandoned on the way to the city, for some reason. They had to be brought in from the other side of the lake — and that's a pretty amazing feat considering the size and weight of the stones." He looked at his two passengers. "When the Spaniards asked the local Aymaras how the city had been constructed, they said the stones were moved with the help of the gods."

A little farther on, Jonathan parked the Land Rover and they scrambled out eagerly, to enter the enclosed site of the ancient ruins. There were a few tourists wandering about in ones or twos, but most were being herded around in big groups by their guides.

Jonathan pointed to a vast mound of earth.

"That's the Akapana Pyramid," he told them. "There's not much of the original structure left now — most of the stones were taken away and used in the village."

More impressive to Olly's mind were the wide, red stone walls that stretched away to the right of the pyramid. Jonathan explained that they surrounded the Kalasasaya — a ritual platform where important ceremonies took place.

They climbed the broad steps, passing between massive stone towers and under a huge square doorway. The sheer size and weight of the immense structure made Olly feel small and frail. It was easy for her to imagine that this was a city built with the help of the gods.

They came into a wide inner courtyard scattered with fallen stone blocks, from which a second stairway led them to another plateau. A big stone doorway stood imposing and solitary at the end of this platform — but it was an entryway without a purpose, for it seemed to lead from nowhere to nowhere.

Olly walked toward it, curious. It was shaped from a single block of stone that towered above her. The crosspiece at the top of the gateway was covered in intricate carvings, and above that was a stylized human figure, its strange, square face staring out over the land as it must have done for thousands of years.

The carved forehead was wrinkled, as though deep in thought. Olly gazed up at it, imagining the amazing sights it must have seen when the city was alive, and wondering what it had been thinking about since the city had fallen and the people had vanished.

"The Gateway of the Sun," Jonathan announced.

Olly jumped. She had been so mesmerized by the ancient stone face, that Jonathan's voice surprised her. She turned away from the face the spell of its outlandish features broken.

"The people who built this temple worshipped the sun," Jonathan told her. "They believed that it rose every morning from the Island of the Sun in Lake Titicaca."

"And at night the moon rose from the Island of the Moon," Josh added.

Olly nodded. "Where's Dad?" she asked.

"At Puma Punku," Jonathan said, pointing away over the ruins. "It's not part of the main site. We'll go there now."

Olly and Josh followed Jonathan out of the enclosed site and across a railway line.

"Puma Punku means Gateway of the Puma,"

Jonathan explained. "We think it may have been a wharf. Lake Titicaca was much bigger two and a half thousand years ago, when Tiahuanaco was built. Then it came right up to the city."

As breathtaking as the main site had been, Olly found the sights that met her at Puma Punku more awesome still. It was an area of immense stone slabs — huge beyond belief. They looked as if they had once been a building, until a giant hand had come smashing down on them, breaking them into a jagged heap of rubble.

"The largest stone here weighs an estimated four hundred and forty tons," Jonathan said. "We have absolutely no idea how the stones were moved."

"With the help of the gods," Josh murmured.

Jonathan smiled. "Possibly," he agreed. "And if they weren't moved by magic, then it was certainly a technology we know nothing about. The quarry they come from is nearly twenty miles away." He led them to a small area that had been cordoned off with yellow tape.

"Hi, Dad!" Olly called, catching sight of her father, who was squatting on the ground a little way off, hunched over a notebook. He was surrounded by chips and fragments of stone.

There was no response. It was not until they reached the professor's side that he became aware of their presence.

"Found the missing piece yet?" Olly asked.

Her father straightened up, shaking his head. "None of these pieces are made from the same type of stone as the slab," he said, gesturing at the rubble that surrounded them. "This is all sandstone and basalt, but the Puma Punku stone is granite."

"Can we see it?" Josh asked.

Professor Christie pointed to the far corner of the taped-off area. A dark-gray slab of stone lay on the ground, broken at the bottom right-hand corner. The two friends went over to look at it, leaving Jonathan and the professor deep in conversation.

Olly knelt to examine the carvings that covered the entire face of the Puma Punku Stone. The slab was about three feet high, and half that wide. A border ran around the edges, divided into squares. The rest of the stone was carved with a grid of different symbols that, for those who could read it, told the story of Coyata's flight with the Amulet of Quilla.

Olly had read books explaining how the ancient people of this area related stories and legends with these stylized pictures — but she couldn't remember enough to be able to translate the carvings herself. She ran a finger along the broken lower edge of the stone. It was maddening to think that the answer to their search was missing. "Do you think it would do any good to dig around a little here?" she asked Josh. "Just in case?"

He didn't reply. She looked around and up at him. He was staring at the stone with a curious expression on his face — almost as if he couldn't quite believe his eyes.

"Are you OK?" she asked.

"Stand up," he told her. "You're too close."

Puzzled, she got to her feet.

Josh pulled her a step back from the stone. "Look!"

"At what?" Olly asked.

"Just *look*!" Josh told her, urgently.

She looked. For a few moments, she stared down at the stone without understanding what it was that had caught Josh's eye. But then the pattern of carvings along the border began to remind her of something.

The main intricate design was edged with a deep double groove and surrounded by a border of squares. Some of the squares contained squat, stylized human figures, with their arms raised in different positions.

Olly's eyes widened and her hand flew to her mouth as realization dawned. "Josh — it can't be!" she gasped.

"I think it is," Josh replied.

"The pattern on the stone is the same . . ." Olly went on.

"Yes."

". . . as the pattern on the mantra in Fabiola's house!" she finished.

"*Yes!*"

Olly's head was swimming. She took a long, deep breath to calm herself. "OK," she said slowly. "Let's see if I've got this right. The patterns inside the border tell the story of Coyata's escape from the Island of the Moon — and explain where she took the Amulet of Quilla, right?"

Josh nodded.

"And the reason Dad can't work out where she took the amulet is because the bottom corner of the stone is missing." She stared at her friend, her voice bursting with excitement. "But Josh — Fabiola's mantra has the complete pattern. The design must have been copied from the stone way back when it was still in one piece. We have to tell Dad!"

Josh caught her sleeve. "Wait," he said. "The pattern on the mantra is very similar to this, but I'm not sure that it's *exactly* the same."

"Of course it is!" Olly said. "It's got those little men with the crooked arms and everything."

"The little men aren't important," Josh pointed out. "It's the writing on the rest of the stone that matters."

"I think it's the same," Olly said, sounding less certain now. "Don't you?"

"I think so," Josh replied, his voice maddeningly calm. "It certainly looks very similar. But we have to be absolutely sure that the two patterns match before we say anything. We don't want to go rushing up to your dad like a couple of excited kids, and then have him say: 'Oh, yes, I noticed that. Actually it's not the same at all'."

Olly nodded, her enthusiasm waning a little. "You're right," she agreed. "So, what do we do?"

"We take some pictures of Fabiola's mantra," Josh said, his eyes gleaming. "Then, we check them against the pictures that Jonathan took of the Puma Punku Stone — they're all on the computer. If the pictures match, we show them to Jonathan and your dad, and look like geniuses!"

Olly thought for a moment and grinned. It was

a good plan. "OK," she said. She looked at her watch. It was three o'clock. She glanced over to where Jonathan and her father were deep in discussion. "But we're not going to get away from here for hours," she sighed. "And by the time we get back, Fabiola's place will probably be closed for the day. Then we have lessons in the morning," she looked at Josh, "which means that we won't be able to check whether we're right till tomorrow afternoon!" Her voice trembled slightly. "Josh — my brain will explode into a million tiny pieces if we have to wait that long. It really will."

"We can't make our own way back though," Josh said. "We have to wait till Jonathan and your dad have finished — unless you have any bright ideas."

Olly frowned. "Well, I have had a stomachache ever since we left the house," she said. "It's not too bad, that's why I didn't mention it. But I could pretend it's worse than it really is and ask Jonathan if he'd mind taking me home."

"It sounds like a plan to me," Josh said.

Olly grinned, then clutched her stomach and tried to look as mournful as possible. "Here goes . . ."

～～～

Olly's grandma was sitting on the veranda when they arrived back at Jazmine's house.

"That was quick," she said, as the three of them came up the steps. She looked sharply at Olly, who was still doing her best to look more ill than she really felt. "Is something wrong?"

"Olly's not feeling very well," Jonathan told her. "A stomach flu, or something."

Mrs. Beckmann became very brisk and efficient. She sat Olly in a chair on the veranda with a cool drink at her side. "I'm sure you'll feel better soon if you just sit quietly," she said firmly.

"Thanks, Gran," Olly replied, feeling a little guilty about the undeserved attention she was getting. But it would be worth it, she thought. They were back in town, and that evening, when they showed Jonathan and her dad a photograph of Fabiola's mantra, she'd be forgiven for overplaying her illness — she hoped.

Once Jonathan was sure that Olly was OK, he headed back to Tiahuanaco. Josh sat down beside Olly, and they both tried to be patient.

After half an hour, Olly decided it was safe to say she felt better and to suggest to her grandma that she and Josh go into town. Mrs. Beckmann wasn't convinced that this was such a good idea, but Olly was persuasive. "I feel fine now," she said. "I think a walk would do me good."

"Very well," Mrs. Beckmann agreed. "But if you feel the slightest twinge, I want you to come straight back. And in any event, I want you back here by six o'clock."

Olly nodded. "Don't worry," she assured her. "We will be."

Her grandma went back into the house.

Olly looked at Josh. "That wasn't too tricky," she murmured. "Now, let's go."

"I just have to get my camera," Josh said, bounding up the steps.

Olly sat on the bottom stair while she waited for him to come back. She crossed her fingers. "Please, please, please," she whispered, her eyes tight shut. "Please let the patterns be exactly the same."

〰〰

"Josh! Olly! How lovely to see you again!" Fabiola beamed at them, her dark eyes sparkling. She looked searchingly past the friends as they stood in the doorway. "Is Audrey with you?"

"No," Olly said. "We've come on our own this time." She looked at Fabiola. "We're on a mission."

Fabiola gazed at her in surprise.

"We'd like to take a few pictures of one of the mantras you showed us yesterday," Josh put in, taking the small digital camera out of its pouch. "If that's OK."

"Of course," Fabiola agreed. "Which one?"

"The one you told us your great-grandmother made," Olly said. "You know — the one with the little men all round the edge."

Fabiola gave them a curious look, her hand rising to her mouth.

Sensing a problem, Olly looked across the room. The patch of wall above the door to the courtyard was bare. Olly stared in disbelief at the place where the mantra had once been.

"I'm sorry," Fabiola said. "A man came into the shop only this morning. He was interested in the mantra. I told him that it was not for sale, but he offered me a great deal of money — far, far more than it was worth. I didn't want to sell the mantra — it has great sentimental value for me — but I couldn't refuse so much money. And I do have other things woven by my great-grandmother." She looked from Olly to Josh. "I'm sorry, but he took the mantra away with him. It's gone."

Chapter Six:
Fire!

It took a few moments for the truth to sink into Josh's brain. The vital mantra was sold! Gone!

"Do you have another mantra with the same pattern?" Olly asked anxiously.

"No," Fabiola replied. "It was a very old design. I doubt if there is another like it in the entire town." She looked at the two friends. "I thought that was why the man was so insistent on buying it — and why he paid so much money."

"Do you have a copy of the pattern?" Josh inquired.

Fabiola shook her head. "I'm afraid not. The design is not used these days — people prefer more straightforward patterns."

Olly was standing with her eyes closed, swaying slightly. "This isn't happening," she murmured under her breath. "This is *not* happening!"

"What is wrong?" Fabiola asked, looking puzzled. "There are many other beautiful mantras." She gestured around the walls. "Could you not take photographs of them?"

Josh took a deep breath. "That one was kind of special," he explained. "I don't suppose you know the name of the man who bought it? We'd really like to find him, if possible."

"Certainly, I do," Fabiola replied. "I wrote it down in our sales book."

Hopeful, Josh and Olly followed Fabiola to a desk in one corner of the room. She pulled a battered old ledger out of a drawer and laid it open on the table.

"There," she said, pointing at an entry near the bottom of the page. "His name is Benedito da Silva, and he is staying at the Hotel El Ray." She smiled at them. "It is a very good hotel — the best in town. Señor da Silva, he was a foreigner. He spoke no Spanish. We talked together in English, but he had a strong Portuguese accent. I would say he is a Brazilian gentleman."

"The Hotel El Ray," Josh repeated. He looked at Fabiola. "Can you tell us how to get there?"

"Of course," Fabiola responded. "It is easy. Turn right from here and follow the road. The hotel is at the far end. You can't miss it. But you may be too late — Señor da Silva told me he was leaving town today. He said he was catching an airplane from La Paz. He may have left already."

Olly let out a gasp of dismay.

"Thanks for everything," Josh called back to Fabiola as he and Olly darted to the door. They took a sharp right turn and raced along the street as if their lives depended on it.

~~~~~

The Hotel El Ray was an imposing Spanish colonial building several stories tall, set in the more modern part of the town. A uniformed man stood at the entrance. He gave the two friends a disapproving look as they came hurtling up the wide stone steps and flew in through the open doors.

Josh glanced around the impressive foyer. The décor was Spanish-influenced, the ornate architecture gilded with gold leaf. Wide, sweeping stairways led to the upper floor.

"There!" Olly gasped, pointing to a long curved reception desk. A young woman eyed them curiously from behind the desk as they ran over to her. "*Buenas tardes*," she said politely as they almost cannoned into the desk.

"*¿Dónde está Señor Benedito da Silva?*" Olly pronounced carefully. *Where is Mr. Benedito da Silva?*

The receptionist replied with a stream of Spanish that Josh didn't understand.

Olly shook her head. "*¿Habla inglés?*" she asked hopefully. *Do you speak English?*

"Certainly," the young woman responded. "I asked whether you can tell me in which room Señor da Silva is staying."

"We don't know," Olly told her frantically. "But he's definitely staying here."

"Could you check your books?" Josh asked. "It's really very important."

The receptionist nodded. With agonizing slowness she flicked through a stack of file cards. "Yes," she said at last. "Señor da Silva is in room two-one-four."

"Thanks," said Olly as she headed for the stairs. "That's all we need to know!"

"Please wait!" the young woman called. "If you wish to speak with Señor da Silva, I will call him." She gestured for them to stay where they were, while she picked up the phone and punched in some numbers.

"Hello, Señor da Silva," she said into the phone. "I have two young people here who wish to speak with you." She listened for a few moments. "Very well, sorry to have troubled you," she finished and put the phone down.

"Señor da Silva cannot see anyone now," she told Olly and Josh. "He is preparing to leave. He has to take a taxi to La Paz Airport. He has no time. I am sorry."

"We only need to see him for a few minutes," Josh pleaded.

The young woman shook her head. "It is not possible."

"Can't you call him again?" Olly begged.

The young woman frowned. "No," she said firmly. "I am very sorry, but Señor da Silva cannot be disturbed."

Temporarily defeated, the two friends headed back to the street.

Olly stared thoughtfully at the hotel doors. "We've got to see him, somehow, Josh," she murmured. "We have to get a photo of that mantra."

"Perhaps if we wait here till he comes out," Josh suggested. "We can explain everything to him in person. I'm sure he'll let us take just one photo."

Olly shook her head. "You've got to be kidding," she said. "We can't tell him that the mantra he just bought holds the secret to finding the priceless Amulet of Quilla."

Now that Olly had spelled it out, Josh realized it

probably wasn't such a good plan. But what else could they do?

"Wait here," Olly said suddenly. "I have an idea."

Before Josh could reply, Olly jogged to the corner of the hotel and darted out of sight down a side alley. Josh stared after her, wondering what she was planning. He walked to the end of the alley and waited for her to come back.

"Josh! Quick!" He turned his head to see Olly leaning out of a side entrance to the hotel, beckoning him urgently. He hurried over to her.

"I think this must be the worker's entrance or something," she said. "But from here, we can make our way up to the main rooms."

"How does that help, if Mr. da Silva won't let us in?" Josh asked.

"Come with me," Olly replied with a crafty grin.

Josh followed her into a small hallway, where she pointed to something on the wall. It was a small red box with a round glass panel in it.

"See?" Olly said triumphantly.

"It's the fire alarm," Josh remarked. "So what?"

"So, what happens when a fire alarm goes off?" Olly prompted.

"There's a mad rush to get out of the building," Josh said. Then he stared at her, suddenly realizing what she had in mind. "No!" he said adamantly. "Olly, we can't set off the alarm. People will think the place is on fire."

"Yup!" Olly agreed cheerfully. "And the hotel will be completely deserted until they realize that it isn't. That'll give us time to get up to Mr. da Silva's room and photograph the mantra."

"But what if he takes it with him?" Josh asked.

Olly frowned. "Josh, if a fire alarm goes off, you don't stop to collect your luggage, you run for it. Trust me — this will be easy. We'll be in and out of his room in thirty seconds."

Josh looked at her doubtfully. But he saw that familiar, dogged glint in her eye that meant she wouldn't take no for an answer. He sighed and nodded.

Olly stepped up to the fire alarm. She lifted the small metal rod from its cradle and smashed the glass panel.

For a split second, there was silence. Then the entire hotel erupted with the shrill scream of the alarm. Josh heard the staff shouting at each other. Then Olly grabbed him and pulled him into a space under the stairs, where they ducked down behind a pile of empty sacks.

Josh heard voices approaching, then the clatter of feet rushing down the stairs. He huddled farther down behind the sacks, listening to the confused chatter of Spanish voices as people flooded past his hiding place and out through the side door.

At last, Olly lifted her head to peer over the barrier of sacks.

"I think everyone's gone," she hissed. "Come on. We don't have much time."

She led the way up the stairs to the second floor. A door brought them out into a richly decorated corridor. Several doors to hotel rooms stood open. The fire alarm was still ringing loudly. Olly grinned. The whole floor seemed deserted.

Olly and Josh ran along the corridor, checking the room numbers as they passed. Josh had the horrible feeling that at any moment someone would appear in the corridor and stop them.

"This is it!" Olly said eventually. The door to room two-one-four was wide open. The room inside was luxurious, with a huge double bed and red flock wallpaper. A suitcase lay open on the bed, half filled. Items of clothing lay scattered where Mr. da Silva had left them when the alarm interrupted his packing. Several smaller leather bags stood waiting on the carpet. Draped between the handles of one of them was a roll of woven, colored material.

Olly recognized the mantra and snatched it up. "Got it!" Her eyes shined as she smiled at Josh. "What did I tell you? Am I a genius or what?"

Josh closed the door. The lock clicked. He took his camera out. "Unroll it and hold it up," he said nervously. He wanted to be out of that room as soon as possible. The thought of Mr. da Silva — or some member of the hotel staff — finding them in there was not pleasant.

Olly held the roll up to her chin and let the mantra unfurl.

Josh stared for a moment at the familiar grid of storytelling symbols within the border of squares. They were very similar to the carved patterns on the Puma Punku Stone — but were they *exactly* the same? He simply couldn't tell — the design was far too intricate for him to be sure.

"Josh, take the picture!" Olly said urgently.

Josh held the camera to his eye. He clicked and the flash bleached the room. "I'll take a couple more just to be on the safe side," he said. The camera flashed twice more. "OK. That's it. Let's go."

Olly rolled the mantra up again and put it back

between the handles of the bag. She grinned happily at Josh. "I said it would be easy, didn't I?"

Josh nodded and turned toward the door. He was just reaching for the handle when he saw it move. Above the constant wail of the fire alarm, he heard a man's voice give a sharp, angry exclamation in a foreign language.

Josh turned to Olly in alarm. Her face was frozen in dismay.

The handle rattled again.

Josh backed away from the door. Someone was trying to get into the room — and there was no way for the two of them to get out. The plan had gone spectacularly wrong.

Chapter Seven: ~
The Aerie of the White
Eagle

Josh stared desperately around the hotel room.
He could hear the man outside fumbling with his
room key. In a few seconds he would come bursting
in on them.

Meanwhile, Olly was calmly sliding under the
bed. She looked up and beckoned to him.

Josh dropped to the carpet and squirmed under
the bed to join Olly. She pulled the valance down
straight, making sure that they were completely
hidden.

In the small gap between the valance and the
carpet, Josh could see a thin slice of the room,
including the leather bags, and the stretch of carpet
in front of the door. As he watched, the door opened
and a man stood poised for a moment in the doorway. Josh wriggled quietly into a better position so
he could see the man's face. The newcomer,

presumably Mr. da Silva, was tall and slim with a gaunt, tanned face and a mane of pure white hair. Josh guessed that he was in his fifties or early sixties. He was wearing a white suit, and Josh had the oddest feeling he had seen the man before.

Mr. da Silva ran toward the bed, muttering something in a language Josh didn't understand. A second later, he headed back toward the door. Josh saw him dash through the doorway and vanish into the corridor. He had the rolled-up mantra tucked under his arm.

Josh waited a few seconds to make sure the man was out of earshot before he spoke. "He's gone," he gasped. "Let's get out of here!"

The two friends squirmed out from under the bed and hurried out of the room. They ran along the corridor and tumbled down the back stairs. They paused for a moment at the side entrance, and Josh peered out cautiously, but the coast was clear. The people evacuated from the hotel had gathered at the front. He could see them milling around at the end of the alley.

Josh and Olly slipped out the side door and ran in the opposite direction.

〰〰

"What kind of an idiot runs into a burning building, grabs one thing, and then runs out again?" Olly gasped.

"The building wasn't actually burning," Josh pointed out.

"He didn't know that," Olly responded.

They were seated on a low stone wall in a plaza several streets away from the hotel, catching their breath.

Olly looked at Josh. "Was it Mr. da Silva?" she asked.

"I think so." Josh nodded. "He must have run for his life when he heard the alarm go off. But then for some reason he decided to come back and grab the mantra." He frowned. "Why would he do that?"

"Fabiola said he paid her a small fortune for it," Olly said. "Maybe he didn't want to see his brand new investment go up in smoke."

Josh nodded thoughtfully. "I suppose not."

Olly shoved him. "Well?" she said eagerly. "Have you checked whether the pictures came out?"

Josh took the camera out of its pouch and switched it on. The small back panel lit up. He clicked to review the pictures and saw tiny, bright images of Olly holding the mantra. "Yes," he said, smiling. "We've got it!"

"Great!" Olly declared, grinning back.

"Just one thing, though," Josh added. "I don't think we should tell anyone about what we had to do to get these pictures."

He could imagine how Olly's grandma would react if she knew they'd set off a fire alarm when there was no fire, and then gone sneaking into somebody else's hotel room. Somehow, he didn't think she'd be impressed.

"Good thinking," Olly agreed. "We'll tell Dad and gran that we saw the mantra at Fabiola's place — and let them think we photographed it there." She stood up. "Now let's get back. I want to see the pictures Jonathan took of the Puma Punku Stone — and the look on his face if the symbols on the stone turn out to be the same ones as on the mantra!"

~~~~

Josh and Olly were in Josh's room. Josh sat at the table while Olly perched on the corner watching his every move. The camera was in its cradle, and the cradle wire was plugged into the laptop. They were waiting for the program to open.

"Oh, come on," Olly urged. "Why is it so slow?"

Josh looked at her. "It's only been about five seconds," he said. "Chill out, Olly."

The page opened up on the screen and a series of

small images appeared. Josh clicked the first image, which promptly expanded to fill the screen.

The picture clearly showed Olly standing with her hands up level with her shoulders, the colorful mantra hanging down in front of her body.

"It worked!" Josh cried, rocking back in his chair.

Olly scrutinized the picture. A grin spread over her face — every little detail of the pattern on the mantra was visible. "Well done, Josh," she said. "Now open one of Jonathan's pictures of the Puma Punku Stone, so we can compare the two."

She watched anxiously as Josh found the folder where his brother had put his pictures. There were a lot of them — dozens of pictures of Inak Uyu on the Island of the Moon, and many more of Tiahuanaco. But finally, as Josh scrolled down the page, he came to a set of pictures of the granite Puma Punku Stone.

He enlarged the best one, and they both leaned forward to examine it closely.

"It's the same," Olly breathed at last.

"Is it?" Josh asked. "Are you sure?"

"Of course I'm sure!" Olly declared. "Print them out, Josh. Now!" She bounced off the table and did a triumphant dance around the room. "We did it!

We did it!" she crowed. Then she ran to the window and shouted. "Hey, Ethan Cain, King of the World! You might as well head home! Olly and Josh are way ahead of you!"

The door to Josh's room opened. "For heaven's sake, what's all this noise about?" asked Olly's grandma. "It sounded like a herd of elephants was jumping around up here!"

Olly ran over to her grandma and danced her around the bed. "We need to call Dad!" she said excitedly. "He has to get back here right now! Josh and I have found something amazing!"

～～～

More than an hour had passed. Olly, Josh, Audrey Beckmann, Jonathan, and Professor Christie were seated around the table on the veranda. Jonathan and the professor were staring at the two pictures that Josh had printed out — one picture of Olly holding up Fabiola's mantra, one picture of the broken Puma Punku Stone. The two men seemed flabbergasted.

"They're the same, aren't they?" Olly demanded, unable to wait any longer for Jonathan or her father to speak.

Jonathan didn't take his eyes from the pictures. "Yes, I think they are," he confirmed. "I can't believe it!" He began to laugh. "Why didn't you say something when we were at Puma Punku?"

"We weren't sure that we were right," Olly explained. "We wanted to be absolutely certain before we said anything."

"Can you translate it?" Josh asked eagerly. "Do you know what the missing part says?"

Professor Christie looked up. "Jonathan, would you fetch me Hugo Rojo's book, please? And we'd better have the Poznansky translations, too."

Olly recognized the names — the men were leading authorities on the meanings of Inca and pre-Inca storytelling symbols. Jonathan and her father had been consulting their works extensively both before and during the trip.

Mrs. Beckmann looked sternly at Olly. "I take it that this was why you wanted to go for a walk into the town?" she said. "And why you asked Jonathan to bring you home early?"

Olly nodded sheepishly. "But I really did have a stomachache," she added quickly. "It just wasn't quite as bad as I led you to believe." She gave her grandma a hopeful look. "It was worth it, though, wasn't it?"

Mrs. Beckmann raised an eyebrow. "Hmmm," she murmured dubiously.

Anything further that Olly's grandma might have wished to say on the subject was interrupted by the arrival of a car. Jazmine emerged with some shopping. "It's madness down there," she said, gesturing back toward the town as she came up to the veranda. "Complete chaos!" She slumped into a chair. "It's taken me three quarters of an hour to get through."

Olly gave her an uneasy look. "Why? What's wrong?" she asked.

"Apparently some fool set off the fire alarm in the Hotel El Rey," Jazmine explained. "The whole place was evacuated, and the police and the fire service turned out in force, only to discover it was a false alarm. But the hotel is on the main through-road. It was blocked solid. It'll be hours before things get back to normal."

"Do they know who set the alarm off?" Mrs. Beckmann asked.

Olly winced.

"A couple of kids, apparently," Jazmine replied. "They were seen hanging around the hotel just before the alarm went off."

Olly forced her face into its most innocent expression and tried to look angelic. Out of the corner of her eye, she saw Josh hurriedly lean over the table to examine the photos again. The business with the fire alarm at the Hotel El Rey was one part of the story that neither of the friends was excited to explore.

Mrs. Beckmann frowned. "Some children do the most stupid, thoughtless things," she sighed. She looked at Olly and Josh. "I'm glad you two have more sense."

~~~~~

The night pressed in at the windows of Jazmine's sitting room. It was actually well past the time when Mrs. Beckmann would usually have suggested Olly and Josh go to bed, but everyone was still up.

Jazmine was seated at one end of the room, quietly playing the guitar. Olly's grandma was seated in an armchair, reading. And Olly and Josh were playing Scrabble. But Olly couldn't concentrate — and judging by Josh's pathetic word tally, he was as distracted as she was.

Every few minutes, Olly would glance at the door to the study. Her father and Jonathan had been locked up in there for hours, poring over the text books, examining the photographs of the mantra and the Puma Punku Stone, trying to solve the final piece of the puzzle.

"Squink isn't a word," Josh declared, staring down at the board where Olly had just placed her tiles.

Olly looked at him. "It isn't? Are you sure?"

"Mrs. Beckmann?" Josh called out. "Squink?"

Olly's grandma looked up briefly from her book and shook her head.

"Rats!" Olly said, picking up the tiles again. She let out a deep breath and stared impatiently at the door. This time, her father was standing in the doorway, with Jonathan right behind him.

Olly and Josh both sprang up, the Scrabble game forgotten.

"Well?" Olly demanded.

The guitar fell silent. Mrs. Beckmann looked up from her book.

A grin spread across Jonathan's face. "We've cracked it," he announced. "According to the writing on the lower right corner of the mantra — that's the part missing from the stone — Coyata hid the Amulet of Quilla in the temple known as the Lair of the Anaconda King."

Olly hardly dared ask the next question. "And do you know where that is?"

Her father smiled. "It's beneath an outcrop of rock referred to as the Aerie of the White Eagle."

"We're not exactly sure where the Aerie of the White Eagle is yet," Jonathan put in. "But the writing on the mantra places it in a forested region of the Beni River. Our maps show several outcrops of rock near to the town of Rurrenabaque — the locals call it Rurre — on the Beni River."

The professor nodded, his smile widening. "Rurre is nearly three hundred miles from here, in the northern Bolivian lowlands. We are hoping that the local guides will be able to tell us which of the outcrops is associated with eagles. Once we have that piece of information, we should be well on our way to locating the temple." He looked across the room toward their hostess, his eyes shining. "I'm sorry to have to leave you so abruptly, Jazmine," he said. "But tomorrow morning we hope to take a flight from La Paz to Rurre."

Olly wasn't sure whether it was she, Josh, or Jonathan who let out the loudest yell of triumph. The hunt for the Amulet of Quilla was on!

Chapter Eight: A Dangerous Road

Olly woke early the next day, filled with excitement and anticipation. She dressed quickly and went out onto the balcony. The air was still cool under the shadow of the roof, but the sky was bright and clear and promised another fine, hot day. She leaned on the parapet and looked out over the town. Beyond the buildings and the brown parched hills, Lake Titicaca shined like sapphire as the upper rim of the sun cleared the mountains, filling the great valley with shimmering light.

She walked along to Josh's room. He was up already, too, sitting on his bed with the laptop on his knees.

"Mom has sent another e-mail," he told Olly. "She's in a place called Alice Springs." He turned the laptop to show Olly a map of Australia's Northern Territory. "It's in the middle of a desert, apparently," he added.

"Did she mention Ethan?" Olly asked.

"She says they've spoken on the phone a couple of times," Josh replied.

"And is he in California?"

Josh shrugged. "She doesn't say." He looked at Olly. "But I'm not going to tell Mom where we're going," he said. "Not just yet." He frowned. "Maybe we've got it wrong, and Ethan isn't coming here at all, but . . ."

"But if he is," Olly finished for him. "It would be better if your mom wasn't able to tell him the latest news." She nodded. "Good thinking."

A moment later, the door opened and Audrey Beckmann looked into the room.

"Ah, here you both are," she said.

Olly frowned at her. "Not schoolwork — not this morning?" she said.

"No. No lessons," her grandma replied.

"You see, we have to pack and stuff," Olly continued persuasively. "And I was . . . Oh! What did you say?"

"No lessons today," Mrs. Beckmann told her, smiling. "Breakfast is ready."

Olly and Josh looked at each other.

Olly grinned. "Excellent!" she said. "This is going to be a perfect day. Off to La Paz Airport. An airplane to Rurre. And by evening we'll be in the middle of the rain forest! Very exciting!"

~~~~~

On their way out to the veranda, where the table was set for the usual breakfast of orange juice and sweet pastries, they passed Jonathan. He was sitting on the stairs and speaking into the phone. His Spanish was fluent, and Olly could only make out a few words here and there, but from the look on his face and the tone of his voice, she guessed that he was speaking to someone at La Paz Airport — and that the conversation was not going well.

Jazmine, Audrey Beckmann, and Olly's father were already outside. The professor's part of the table was scattered with open books and documents. Olly and Josh sat down and began to eat.

It was about ten minutes later that Jonathan emerged from the house. "It's not good news," he said, sounding exasperated. "As far as I can make out, the baggage handlers are on strike at the airport. No planes can land or take off till the dispute's been settled."

Professor Christie looked at him anxiously. "And have you any idea how long that will take?" he asked.

"The woman on the phone said, 'mañana,'" Jonathan replied.

"That means 'tomorrow,'" Olly said. "That's not too bad."

Jazmine shook her head. "We don't always mean tomorrow when we say *mañana*," she told them. "It can mean tomorrow, or the day after, or next week, or next month."

Professor Christie frowned. "I have to be back in England in eight days," he said. "We can't afford a delay."

"Can't we go by road?" Josh asked.

"There is one road north through the mountains," Jazmine said, "but I would not recommend it."

"Have you any idea how long this dispute might last?" Audrey Beckmann asked Jazmine.

"I will make some calls," Jazmine said. She got up and went into the house.

She was only gone a few minutes, but the look on her face when she returned was not encouraging. "I'm afraid the strike will not be over quickly," she declared. "Negotiators are expected in the next few days — but the talks could take days or even weeks."

"Then we will have to travel by road," sighed the professor.

"I'll hire a van," Jonathan said.

Olly looked curiously at Jazmine. "Why did you say you didn't recommend the road?" she asked.

Jazmine hesitated for a moment before answering. "The only way to travel north from here is to take the mountain road that leads from La Paz to Coroico," she explained. "The people of these parts have a name for that road — they call it *El Peligroso.*"

Jonathan frowned at her. "That just means 'dangerous,'" he said.

Jazmine nodded. "It has a bad reputation," she warned. "It is a gravel road that goes down the mountains. It is little more than ten feet wide, and there is a drop of many hundreds of feet on one side."

"Wow!" Olly exclaimed. "That sounds cool!"

Jazmine looked at her. "About twenty-six vehicles a year are lost on that road," she said somberly. "That is one every two weeks. I do not think you will be so happy once you see *El Peligroso.*"

Olly and Josh exchanged a glance. It *was* a little unnerving to have to take such a notorious road, but it struck Olly that the journey to Rurre was going to be exciting to say the very least.

"Woah!" Olly breathed.

"Is *that* the road?" Josh asked, sounding awe-struck.

Audrey Beckmann's eyes widened and her back became a little stiffer.

Professor Christie was too busy with a lapful of documents to even look up.

Jonathan pressed his lips together, but said nothing.

They were in a battered, dusty old minivan, hired in La Paz. They had left the busy city behind them some time ago, and traveled out into the mountains. The road was rough and uneven, but at first there had been no sign of the dangerous cliff edges Jazmine had mentioned. Then they had rounded a towering outcrop of rust-colored rock. A stunning sight had opened out ahead of them.

They were on the crest of a steep-walled valley, plunging down through the parched mountains. Olly gazed along the road ahead as it started to descend from the crest, winding down the valley wall, like a thin white scar cut into the sheer mountainside.

From this point, the high ridges of the Altiplano

tumbled down in crags and peaks to the distant lowlands of the Amazon Basin — hazy and blue on the very edge of the horizon.

Olly could see tiny vehicles moving up and down the road, seeming to cling, like ants, to the rock-face.

Jonathan only hesitated for a moment. "Here goes nothing," Olly heard him mutter under his breath, and then he drove over the crest and down onto the steep, narrow mountain road.

The scenery was breathtaking — towering cliffs of sunburned, red rock reared up around them, arid and scorched by the brutal sun.

The road zigzagged slowly downward. Olly leaned out of the window and stared into the dizzying chasm. Usually, she had no fear of heights, but the immensity of this fall dried her mouth and made the hairs on the back of her neck stand on end.

Jonathan was hunched over the steering wheel, peering ahead, his face tight with concentration. Olly's father was speechless in the seat beside him. The most unnerving moments came when they had to move out onto one of the broader turning points in the road, to allow ascending vehicles to pass them. At these times, Jonathan had to take the van to the very brink of the cliff, the wheels only a foot and a half from the crumbling edge. Then they had to wait, holding their breath, as a truck rumbled past — shaking the ground and filling the air with choking red dust — before they could move back into the middle of the road and continue their journey.

Jonathan wiped sweat out of his eyes. Even with all the windows open, the van was becoming uncomfortably hot. Mrs. Beckmann handed out bottled water as they continued to crawl down through the mountains.

Olly leaned farther out, gazing in fascination into the gulf. Far, far below, she saw the tangled, rusted wreckage of a truck. She thought of the poor people who had been in the vehicle, and swallowed hard. Then she felt her grandma's hand grip her shoulder and pull her back into the seat.

"Not so far out, Olly, please," Mrs. Beckmann said quietly.

They crept around a wide shoulder of rock. Olly could see the road plunging ahead, empty of oncoming traffic. "How much farther is Coroico?" she asked.

Josh had a map spread open on his lap. "It's difficult to tell," he replied. "Coroico is about eighty miles from La Paz. I think we've gone about halfway." He looked up. "What's that noise?" he asked, frowning.

Olly listened. She could hear the growl of the engine and the crunch and grind of the wheels on the gravel track, but Josh was right, there was a new sound — a distant rumble, like prolonged thunder.

She stared up through the dusty windscreen into the clear, blue sky. And then the whole world turned red and the roof of the van began to clang and echo with the terrifying impact of a hundred small stones. Through the enveloping cloud of dust, Olly could see rocks and stones spilling down over them, bouncing off the hood and cracking on the windshield. They ricocheted and scattered as they came hurtling down from some unguessable height. Some were just small pebbles, but others were much bigger. They crashed down onto the van like hammer blows as it rocked and shuddered under the impact.

Jonathan flicked the windshield wipers on and fought with the wheel, his foot hard on the break, his face strained and ashen as he labored to keep the van under some kind of control. The wipers struggled to sweep the debris away, but more and more poured down to replace it. The roar and thunder of the rockfall was deafening.

Olly could hear her father shouting something —

and her grandma and Josh, too, but their voices were all drowned out by the terrible noise of the rocks on the roof. She let out an involuntary scream as she saw a boulder smash into the road only a foot and a half ahead of them. Never in her life had she been so utterly terrified.

Jonathan spun the wheel, desperately trying to avoid crashing into the boulder, but anxious not to drive over the edge of the mountain at the same time. Unfortunately, the rubble on the road was moving under the van's wheels, and he could not get any traction.

Olly hung on grimly as one wheel hit the boulder with a bone-jarring crack and the back of the van began to slide away. Dust cascaded in through the open window, filling her nose and mouth and stinging her eyes. The rockfall was pushing the van to the outside edge of the road, and through a sudden gap in the avalanche of dust and stones, she saw the abyss yawning only inches away from them.

The wheels spun. The engine roared shrilly. The van teetered on the very brink of the mountain, and under the constant hammering of falling rocks, it slowly began to tip up. Olly clung to her seat and closed her eyes in terror. The van was slithering over the precipice.

Chapter Nine:
Journey's End

"Everyone, over to this side!" Jonathan shouted above the clamor, his voice cracking with fear.

Olly threw herself across the van, squeezing herself against Josh so she could grab on to the door handle next to her grandma, whose arm was tight around them both. In the front, the professor grasped the back of Jonathan's seat as his assistant leaned toward the window and wrenched at the steering wheel.

Olly saw the shock and panic in their faces. But their combined weight worked a miracle. The van righted itself, and the wheels found some traction on the gravel road. There was a violent shudder, and suddenly the van leaped forward, back onto the road.

A few seconds later they had pressed beyond the rockfall and Jonathan brought the van to a halt. He leaned against the steering wheel, cradling his head in his arms. Olly could see the sweat dripping from his face.

"Well done, Jonathan. Well done!" gasped the professor, patting his assistant on the back.

"Is everyone all right?" asked Olly's grandma, her voice trembling.

Josh had squirmed around in his seat to stare out through the filthy rear windshield. "That was close!" he exclaimed.

Behind them, the road was strewn with rocks and boulders and drifts of rust-colored silt. A cloud of red dust still hung in the air.

Jonathan lifted his head and peered over his shoulder. "No one else is going to be traveling this road today," he remarked. "It's completely blocked."

Suddenly Olly needed to get out of the van. She wrestled with the handle and threw the door open. Then she jumped down onto the gravel road and fell to her knees, panting wildly. Her legs felt like jelly, and her stomach was turning over and over.

"Olly? Are you all right?" Olly opened her eyes at the sound of her grandma's voice. "Look at you — you're filthy. Here, drink this." A bottle of water appeared under her nose.

Olly realized her mouth was desert-dry. She took a swig of water.

"Better?" her grandma asked, smiling.

Olly nodded, her spirits beginning to revive a little. "Yes, thanks." She clambered to her feet.

Jonathan and Professor Christie had gotten out of the van. They were circling the vehicle, checking for damage.

Josh jumped down to join Olly. "I thought we were going over the edge," he said, his voice slightly shrill. "Look at the size of some of those rocks!" He walked toward the debris.

"Josh, keep away from there," Mrs. Beckmann called sharply.

Josh crouched and picked up a small rock that fit into his hand. He stood up and held it out. "A souvenir," he declared.

Olly gazed at him. "Were you scared?" she asked.

He nodded. "You?"

She laughed. "Just a bit!"

"I think it would be a good idea for us to get off this road as quickly as possible," Olly's grandmother called to the two men. "Is the van all right?"

"I think so," Jonathan replied. "It's got a few more dents than it had before, but the tires are OK."

They all climbed back into the van. Olly instantly felt apprehensive. She swallowed hard, determined to master her fear.

Jonathan turned the key in the ignition. The motor coughed into life. The noise made Olly jump. She bit her lip and clenched her fists in her lap.

"So far, so good," Jonathan said. He put the van into gear and they began to move.

The gravel road took them around an outcrop of rock, and the site of the rockfall disappeared. Olly heaved a sigh of relief.

A few minutes later, they skirted another jutting rock, and Olly saw the rooftops of a small town, no more than two miles ahead of them, perched on the side of the mountains. And beyond the town lay great forested canyons and green valleys stretching away into the distance. They had reached Coroico. They had descended six thousand feet out of the Altiplano, and they had survived *El Peligroso* — the most dangerous road in the world.

Olly grinned around at everyone. "Well, that was a piece of cake," she said. "Anyone want to do it again?"

～～～

They arrived in Coroico in the early afternoon and found a quiet, friendly restaurant where they could have a good meal and take some time to recover from their ordeal on the road.

As they ate, Mrs. Beckmann studied a travel guide, and Jonathan and the professor discussed plans for the next stage in the search for the amulet. Josh and Olly talked rapidly together, reliving the perilous journey and the rockfall.

"If one of those big chunks of rock had hit us, it would have gone right through the roof," Josh said cheerfully as he forked up his pasta. "We'd have been pulped!"

"Not while I'm eating, please," Mrs. Beckmann said. "We're going to have to start using bug spray from now on," she added. "There are some extremely unpleasant bugs in these parts."

Olly laughed. "After what we've just been through, insects don't bother me."

"They will if you get stung, Olivia," her grandma said severely. She read from the guidebook. "'The bites of infected mosquitoes can cause malaria, the symptoms of which include loss of appetite, fever, chills, and sweating. If it is not treated quickly, it can prove fatal.'"

Olly blinked at her. "Bring on the bug spray!" she exclaimed.

~~~~~~

The rest of the afternoon was spent driving out of the mountains and through the lush Bolivian lowlands. Occasionally, white mists rose from the deep, forested valleys. The warm, dry air of the Altiplano was being replaced by a humid, stifling heat that sent the sweat running in rivulets down their faces.

But the landscape that unfolded around them made the discomfort of the hot van bearable. They passed through wide orchards of oranges and lemons, and dense coffee plantations dotted with small, picturesque villages. Rivers tumbled through forested gorges, breaking into sparkling waterfalls wrapped secretively in ribbons of mist.

As the afternoon waned, they came out of the hills and began the final stretch of their long journey. Now, they were driving through endless green pampas grass, past cattle ranches and logging operations that had made great, unsightly holes in the rain forest.

It was already evening when they caught their first glimpse of the Rio Beni. It spread out below the road like a glittering black ribbon, winding between thickly forested banks. And then the road crested a final broad hill, and suddenly they were looking down on the town of Rurrenabaque. The sun was setting like a ball of red fire in a sky streaked with gold and orange and purple. The river was cloaked in a blanket of white fog, and the lights of the town twinkled invitingly.

Their long journey was at an end — they had reached the tropical rain forests of the Amazon Basin. The next stage of the hunt for the Amulet of Quilla was about to begin.

~~~~~

Josh woke with a start. He had been dreaming he was back in the van. Rocks and rubble were raining down on it, and then he was falling. . . .

He sat up, trembling slightly. It was pitch dark. Frogs croaked in chorus outside his bedroom window. But he was safe. There were no rocks.

He remembered the drive through Rurre, the climb to the hill behind the town, and being greeted at the door of the hacienda by a friendly European woman. They had cleaned up and eaten a quick meal before being shown to their rooms. Then, exhausted by the long journey, he had thrown his clothes off and fallen into bed.

He lay back again on the soft pillows, and listening to the singing frogs, he soon fell into a dreamless sleep.

~~~~~

Early the next morning, Josh stood on his balcony, gazing down in delight at the broad, silver-blue

Rio Beni as it flowed north through the forested hills. The hacienda where they were staying was to the north of the town, perched on an outcrop of rock that overhung the river. The beautiful rain forest seemed to stretch on forever — fading away into misty blue distances under the burning white sun. The air was filled with the scents of the forest.

The frog chorus was gone, but Josh could hear other noises — now the shrill shriek of birds, the rustle of the warm wind in the trees, the splash of animals in the water, the call of creatures deep in the forest. The whole place teemed with life.

Beautiful orange and black butterflies fluttered on the breeze like tiny kites. A toucan sailed by on outstretched wings, its head and chest vivid splashes of yellow against the blue sky, its huge beak patterned with all the colors of the rainbow.

Josh tore himself away from the view and ran downstairs to join the others in a wide, airy dining room.

"Here he is, at last," said Jonathan.

"We were wondering if you were ever going to wake up," Olly muttered, her mouth full of food. She pointed to a plate of sweet pastries. "Try one of these — they're amazing!"

Josh sat down beside Mrs. Beckmann, who was

there sipping coffee and reading her travel guide. Just then, their hostess came gliding into the room, a slim young woman with long black hair and dark eyes. Her name was Katerina. She smiled at Josh and poured him some fresh juice.

"Where's your dad?" Josh asked Olly as he started eating.

"He's gone off to talk to some local guides," Olly replied. "He shouldn't be long." Her eyes gleamed. "And then we can all head off into the jungle to find the amulet!"

"We'll have to see about that," said Mrs. Beckmann, and Josh noticed that her voice sounded strangely weary.

He looked at her curiously. She did seem a bit pale, and there were dark circles under her eyes.

"Are you OK, gran?" Olly asked.

"I'm fine, Olly," Mrs. Beckmann replied. "Just a little tired."

Katerina gently rested her hand against Mrs. Beckmann's forehead. "I think you have a little touch of fever," she said.

Olly stared at her. "Fever?" she repeated anxiously. "Gran — you haven't been bitten by a mosquito, have you?"

"I don't think so," said her grandma, laughing. She smiled at Katerina. "The journey was a little wearing," she said. "I think maybe I'll lie down for a bit."

"That's a good idea," Katerina agreed.

Mrs. Beckmann lifted herself out of her chair. She looked sternly at Olly and Josh. "You two behave yourselves, all right?" she said.

"Of course," Olly replied indignantly.

"I hope you feel better soon," Josh added.

"Thank you, Josh. I'm sure I will," said Mrs. Beckmann as she left the room.

"Don't worry," Katerina told the friends. "I'll make sure she's OK."

A few minutes later, Professor Christie came in. Jonathan and the two friends looked up hopefully. The professor looked pleased.

"Did you find a guide?" Jonathan asked.

Professor Christie sat down and took out a map. Olly and Josh cleared the table so he could open it. "I have hired a man called Sandro," he said. "I met him on my way into town. He was coming up to the hacienda to offer his services to any tourists. He is a local guide, and he seems to know the area very well. I asked him about the Aerie of the White Eagle. He said there are *two* places that fit the description, but only *one* is associated with eagles. It is on this side of the river and has always been known as Eagle Mount by the locals." Professor Christie pointed to the place on the map.

The others leaned over to look.

"That's farther away than we thought," Jonathan commented. "Didn't the writing on the mantra suggest that it would be much closer to the river?"

"Yes," the professor agreed. "But it is still within the bounds of possibility, and it matches the description in all other respects. Sandro says it will take us two and a half days to get there. We will set off tomorrow, but he has warned me that it will be a difficult journey." He looked at the two friends. "I'm sorry, but I'm afraid that means you can't come with us."

Josh's heart sank. It had never crossed his mind that they would be left out of the final stage in the search. The thought of sitting around for five days or more, while Jonathan and the professor were exploring the Lair of the Anaconda King without them, was crushing.

"You can't leave us behind!" Olly exclaimed. "That's not fair."

"I'm very sorry, Olivia," her father said firmly. "But it's going to be a hard trek through dense jungle. It's no place for you and Josh."

"The professor is right," Jonathan said sympathetically. "I know the two of you would love to join us, but this time, you're going to have to be patient."

Josh could see by the look on Olly's face that she felt as disappointed as he did.

They had come all this way, solved the riddle of the Puma Punku Stone — and now, they were going to be left behind at the very end of the quest.

It was almost too much to bear.

Chapter Ten:
The Brazilian Again

It was a depressing day for Olly and Josh. Jonathan and Professor Christie were busy making arrangements for their trip into the jungle. It wouldn't even be possible for those left at the hacienda to keep in contact with them by cell phone; deep in the pathless heart of the rain forest, they would get no reception.

Audrey Beckmann got up in the afternoon, but everyone could see that she wasn't well. She sat quietly in an armchair on the wide veranda that overlooked the river, looking pale and drawn.

Olly was worried. Her grandma was never ill. She fussed over her, bringing her cool drinks and snacks, constantly checking to see if she needed anything.

"Olivia, please, I'm not an invalid," her grandma said. "I feel a bit run-down, that's all."

"Are you sure that's all it is, Mrs. Beckmann?" Jonathan asked. "It's not wise to ignore these things. I've been talking with the professor, and he thinks you should see a doctor."

"You should, gran," Olly urged. "Just to be on the safe side."

The old lady lifted her hands in surrender. "Very well," she said wearily. "I'll see a doctor."

The doctor came that afternoon and saw Mrs. Beckmann in her room.

Olly waited outside anxiously. "What if she's got malaria or some other horrible disease?" she asked Jonathan. It was very disturbing to think of her grandma being ill — she was the person who held things together. Olly couldn't imagine how anything would work properly without her grandma at the helm.

The doctor was a small, well-dressed man with a goatee and bright black eyes. He spoke to the professor while Olly listened. "It is nothing to worry about," he said in thickly accented English. "Mrs. Beckmann has a mild fever. She must rest. I will write a prescription for her. Katerina will get the medicine and ensure she takes it." He smiled at the worried faces. "I believe you will see a great improvement in forty-eight hours."

Olly let out a sigh of relief. "I'll go and sit with her," she said. "I could read to her or something."

She went up to her grandma's room and found her lying in bed, propped up against the pillows.

"The doctor says you're not to lift a finger for two days," Olly said sternly. "And you've got to do as you're told."

Her grandma smiled. "You're the boss," she said quietly.

Olly nodded. "You bet I am," she agreed. "Now, do you want anything to eat or drink?"

"I don't think so," Mrs. Beckmann replied. "Not right now."

"OK." Olly sat down on the side of the bed. "I'll read to you for a while, then." She picked up the book that her grandma had been reading. It was the chronicle of a journey into the jungle made by explorers in the nineteenth century.

Her grandma settled back into the pillows and closed her eyes as Olly began to read.

~~~~

The next day dawned with an eerie beauty. Ghostly sheets of fog had come curling up the river, giving the water a silvery sheen. The fog coiled slowly through the town, too, so that from the hilltop hacienda, the rooftops of Rurre seemed to be afloat on a rolling silver sea. A warm wind raked the forest, making the treetops ripple and rustle in waves.

The cries and calls of animals and birds were

carried on the breeze. Olly watched as a scarlet macaw flew past her balcony, its feathers as bright as newly spilled blood. It let out a cry that made her shiver. Insects danced on the warm air. A huge, shining, blue-and-green dragonfly startled her as it darted past. An iridescent beetle hovered for a moment, then went zigzagging back into the trees.

In less than an hour, Jonathan and her father would set off with their Indian guide. She had taken note of every detail of the trip as they had discussed it. They would strike inland just north of the town, following a clear path at first. But they would soon have to leave the path and head northeast into uncharted jungle. For two and a half days they would hack their way through to the outcrop of rock known as Eagle Mount.

And then they would know if the story on the mantra, copied from the Puma Punku Stone, was true.

Olly sighed. She was sure they would find the Amulet of Quilla. In five or six days, they would step triumphantly out of the jungle, and the quest for another Talisman of the Moon would be over. And she and Josh would have missed it all!

She sighed again, her spirits sinking as she brooded on the injustice of it.

Then she heard Josh's voice calling from somewhere in the hacienda. "Olly! Come on — they're leaving."

She straightened her back and fixed a smile on her face. It was time to wave the adventurers off with as brave a face as she could muster.

〰〰

Later that morning, Olly made sure her grandma was comfortable in bed with fresh water and a book in case she wanted to read. "We'd like to take a look around the town," Olly said. "That's OK, isn't it?"

"Of course," her grandma replied. "Give me my purse; you'll want some money for lunch."

Olly handed the purse over. "Can we have an advance on our allowance — in case we want to buy some souvenirs?" she begged.

Smiling, Mrs. Beckmann handed the money over. "Now then," she said, "no madcap ideas about exploring the jungle." She eyed Olly's lightweight linen trousers and cotton top. "You'll ruin your clothes. Keep to the town and the riverbank. And I want the two of you back here before nightfall, or there'll be trouble."

"No problem," Olly said. "We won't go anywhere near the jungle."

~~~~~

Josh was ready to go when Olly came back downstairs. His digital camera hung in a canvas bag on one shoulder, and he was wearing a loose cotton top and cargo pants with large pockets. The friends set off into Rurre.

The town was an attractive, bustling place, with long, straight, earthen roads running between white adobe buildings. It was a charming mix of the old and the new — with reed-thatched wooden buildings and colorful adobe shops lining the main streets. There were plenty of hotels, restaurants, and cafés to cater to intrepid tourists who came to sample the delights of the surrounding rain forest and to canoe along the Rio Beni.

Olly quickly cheered up as she and Josh wandered through the town. It was impossible for her to stay gloomy in such a lovely place, and she resolved to make the most of a disappointing situation. They made their way down to the river's edge and watched the wide waters flow by. Local children played in the shallows, splashing each other as they swam and dived.

Groups of tourists were also gathered on the riverbank, waiting their turn to climb into the long, slender canoes that would take them on tours up the river. Olly and Josh decided that later on they would also take a canoe ride.

"Did you know that the word *beni* means 'wind' in the local language?" Josh asked. "So the Rio Beni is the River of the Wind."

Olly smiled at him. "You're a mine of information, aren't you?" She frowned. "I'm thirsty," she said. "Let's go and find something to drink."

They made their way back into the town.

"How do you ask for a drink in Spanish?" Josh asked.

"Well, drink is —" Olly began.

"Olly, look!" Josh's fierce whisper stopped her in mid-sentence.

She followed the line of his pointing finger. "What?" she asked, staring blankly at the people on the far side of the broad street.

"It's *him*!" Josh hissed.

Olly searched the crowd for a familiar face. "Him who?" she asked. "What are you talking about?"

"It's Mr. da Silva," Josh told her. "From the hotel. The man in the white suit."

Now Olly saw who Josh meant. The tall, silver-haired man was standing outside a shop. "Are you sure it's him?" Olly asked.

"Of course I am."

"I wonder what he's doing here," she said thoughtfully. "Wasn't he supposed to be catching a flight to Brazil?"

"Exactly!" Josh replied.

Olly blinked at him. "I suppose he must have got caught by the strike," she said, "and decided to travel around a bit until he could get a flight out." She stared hard at the tanned Brazilian. "It's quite a coincidence that he should turn up here, though, isn't it?" she added. "I wonder what he'd say if he knew that the design on that mantra he bought could lead him to a hidden treasure."

Josh looked sharply at her. "What makes you so sure he doesn't know?" he asked.

Olly started. "What?"

"Think about it," Josh continued. "Didn't Fabiola say he was desperate to buy that particular mantra from her? He paid her a lot more than it was worth. Why would he do that?"

"Because he liked it?" Olly offered.

"Maybe," Josh said. "But then he ran back into

the hotel to save it — even though he thought the building was on fire. And now he's *here*, Olly. I bet that's more than just coincidence." Josh's eyes suddenly widened. "I'm such an idiot!" he gasped.

Olly frowned at him. "Why?"

"I just remembered something," Josh told her. "In the hotel room, I had the feeling that I'd seen Mr. da Silva before. And I remember now — he was in the market the day we first went to Fabiola's place. I saw him watching us. I didn't think anything of it at the time — but what if he was deliberately following us?"

"You mean *spying* on us?" Olly breathed. Her eyes narrowed. "You know who would want us spied on, don't you? Ethan Cain!" She looked back at the tall, slim Brazilian.

"But even if he does know about the amulet, he's too late," Josh pointed out. "Jonathan and your dad have already left."

Before Olly could respond, they noticed a short, dark-haired man approach Mr. da Silva and speak to him. Da Silva nodded, then frowned and shook his head. The shorter man spoke again and then the two walked away together.

"I know that man," Josh whispered. "I saw him with Sandro this morning when he came to pick up your dad. I think his name's Lucho. He's a guide, too." He looked at Olly and frowned. "If Mr. da Silva is going to hire Lucho to guide him to the Eagle Mount, he'll only be a few hours behind Jonathan and the professor!"

"Let's find out if that *is* what he's doing," Olly suggested. "Let's spy on the spy!" She darted across the road, with Josh right behind her. Together, the friends trailed the two men as they made their way through the crowds.

When Mr. da Silva and Lucho turned down a side street, Olly and Josh dropped back a little to keep from being spotted. From the corner of the street, they saw the men sit down at a round, white table in front of a café. Tall ferns in terra-cotta pots marked out the forecourt of the café, and Olly figured she and Josh could use these as cover to draw closer to their quarry.

They sneaked toward the café until they were close enough to eavesdrop on Mr. da Silva's conversation. Olly listened intently, ready to try and work out his plans from the small amount of Spanish she understood. But she soon discovered that the conversation was being conducted in English. Mr. da Silva was Brazilian, she remembered. Fabiola had said that he didn't speak Spanish — only

Portuguese. English was obviously the only language that the two men had in common. She grinned happily at Josh.

"When did they leave?" Mr. da Silva was asking.

"Early this morning," Lucho replied. "Sandro will take them far into the forest, do not worry. They will not return for many days — five, maybe six."

Olly stiffened and threw a quick glance toward Josh. He nodded sharply, as if reading her thoughts. The two men were talking about Jonathan and her father.

"You're sure they didn't suspect anything?" Mr. da Silva demanded.

"Yes, quite sure." Lucho said firmly. "Sandro told them that the Aerie of the White Eagle was probably Eagle Mount, which is to the northeast. He did not tell them that the nearer outcrop, overlooking the Rio Beni, is known as Eagle's Nest. Eagle's Nest is sure to be the *real* Aerie of the White Eagle."

Olly's head swam. Sandro had deliberately lied to her father. The Aerie of the White Eagle was really much nearer to the river — just as Jonathan and her dad had first thought.

"It will be many days before they realize that they are looking in the wrong place," Lucho continued. "And by then, your friend will have done what he came here to do. He left yesterday with a team of men. He will be at the Aerie of the White Eagle now."

"I want you to take me there, too," da Silva.

"I will need more money," Lucho told him.

"That's not a problem," replied da Silva. "When can we set off — and how long will it take us to get there?"

"We can set off immediately, if you wish," said Lucho. "And once we have crossed the river, it will only take us three hours to find the place. We will follow the tourist trail for a short distance, then strike out north into the jungle."

"Good," said da Silva. "Finish your coffee. I want to leave immediately."

Olly and Josh backed away as the two men got up from their table and headed off along the street.

Olly was stunned by what she had just overheard. "Dad and Jonathan have been sent in the wrong direction!" she gasped.

"I know," Josh agreed, looking shocked.

"And now Lucho is going to take Mr. da Silva to the *right* place," Olly went on thoughtfully. She turned to her friend. "Let's follow them, Josh! If they lead us to the Aerie of the White Eagle, we may still be able to find the Amulet of Quilla."

Chapter Eleven:
Into the Jungle

Olly stood at the water's edge, one hand up to shield her eyes from the river's silvery glare. There were many crafts on the Rio Beni — a ferry taking tourists to a popular beach upriver, canoes, and small fishing boats. But her attention was focused on one canoe in particular. It was halfway across the river, heading for the far bank.

A sturdy man paddled expertly. In the back of his canoe sat the guide, Lucho, and the tall, silver-haired Brazilian, Benedito da Silva.

"We mustn't lose track of them," Olly said, anxiously.

Josh frowned. "We can't just take off into the jungle, Olly," he said. "We're not really wearing the right kind of clothes. Plus we don't have any water or food."

Olly nodded and pointed to one of the many riverside restaurants. "Go and buy some bottles of water," she said. "I'll hire a canoe."

"And the clothes?" Josh inquired.

"No time."

Josh stared after da Silva's canoe for a moment, then turned and ran up the shoreline.

Olly scanned the riverbank for a canoe to hire. She spotted a skinny young man sitting on the bow of his canoe and hurried over to him.

Josh was right about their clothes, Olly thought, but there wasn't time to go back to the hacienda and change. If they lost sight of Mr. da Silva and his guide, then they might as well forget the whole plan. She knew that once the two men had melted into the jungle, it would be impossible to track them.

She and Josh had to act quickly.

~~~~~

The wiry young man paddled the canoe with ease, and the slender craft cut swiftly across the waters of the Rio Beni. Further along the shoreline, Olly saw a group of capybara wallowing in the shallows, looking a little like furry pigs. Insects circled the canoe, buzzing and whining. Their guide ignored them, but Olly and Josh wasted a lot of energy trying to swat them away. Olly couldn't forget the warning her grandma had read from the guidebook.

As they approached the far bank, Olly spotted

Lucho and da Silva talking with their boatman on the shore. She got the impression they were arguing about money, and she smiled grimly — that delay was exactly what she and Josh needed.

The canoe bumped ashore, and Olly and Josh clambered out. Lucha and da Silva were just disappearing into the trees ahead.

The friends had disembarked in a shallow bay of white stones and brown earth, which sloped gently up to a steep ledge of wiry grass and overhanging trees. They ran up the beach and cautiously entered the forest.

The two men were following a well-worn trail that snaked through the trees. Olly remembered what Lucho had said: They would follow the tourist trail for a while, then head north into the deep jungle. She knew that she and Josh would have to keep their wits about them. They had to keep within tracking distance of the two men, but far enough back so that they wouldn't be spotted.

For half an hour, the two friends followed the men, keeping close to the tree line, ready to duck out of sight if either man should glance back. They met no one else, but the jungle around them was full of life. Olly heard the chirp and whir of insects, the screeching of birds, and the busy rustle of small mammals. Sometimes, a startlingly loud chattering would ring out, and she'd turn in time to see a small golden monkey skittering away through the branches.

Sandflies droned, gathering in whirling clusters under the trees. Olly was glad that they had taken her grandma's advice and covered all their exposed skin with bug spray.

The trail grew narrower — becoming a dark, six-foot-wide tunnel through overhanging trees. There was a series of zigzag bends, following a natural depression in the folded hills.

Olly and Josh jogged from one point of cover to the next — always checking ahead before coming out into the open, until, suddenly, they peered ahead and found that the path was empty.

"They're gone!" Olly whispered. She ran forward, with Josh close behind. There was no sign of the men — it was as if the jungle had just swallowed them up.

"You're in front. Didn't you see where they went?" Josh hissed.

Olly shook her head. She lifted her hand for him to be quiet, and listened intently. The innumerable sounds of the jungle filled her ears — but from close by she heard the distinctive sound of a twig snapping.

She ran off the trail and up a steep ridge, using the tree roots to help her clamber up the slope.

The ridge came to a sharp crest. Olly stared down the slope ahead and grinned. She could just make out da Silva's white jacket through the tangle of green leaves.

She caught hold of Josh's arm as he arrived beside her. She pointed ahead and he nodded. As quickly as they could, they scrambled down from the ridge, trying to move quietly through the undergrowth. Olly could hear the men's voices. She smiled grimly — da Silva seemed to be doing most of the talking, Lucho's voice only drifted back to her now and then.

Olly looked at the forest around her. Progress was a lot slower now that they had left the path, but the jungle was indescribably beautiful. The tree canopy spread out above their heads. The light that filtered through was golden and dappled with shadows. Thick, woody lianas hung from the trees like twisted ropes, and all around, exotic flowers bloomed like pink and crimson stars, their scent sweet and strong. Huge bees hummed as they moved from blossom to blossom, dodging the great sprawling ferns that grew to shoulder height beneath the towering trees. At times, Olly thought, it was like wading through a deep, green sea.

She glanced back at Josh. His face was running with sweat, and striped and smeared with dirt. His hair was sticking to his forehead. She guessed she must look the same.

Olly could no longer see the two men — she was following their disembodied voices. Although she could make out little of what was being said, she got the impression that da Silva was complaining.

Suddenly, she realized that she could hear the conversation more clearly. She caught a glimpse of white through the foliage and stopped quickly. Josh was at her shoulder. Da Silva's voice was belligerent. Lucho sounded apologetic.

"There is no other way," Olly heard him say.

Da Silva let out a curse, and the voices began to move on again.

"What was that about?" Josh whispered.

"I don't know," Olly replied. She pushed through a dense curtain of leaves and almost stepped out into midair. With a stifled gasp, she drew back, clutching onto branches as the ground dropped away at her feet.

She found herself looking down into a steep

ravine, about sixty feet deep — it was as though a giant machete had cut down through the jungle. A tumbling gush of white water ran along the bottom of the cleft. For a moment, Olly was at a loss. There seemed no way across the chasm. But where had Lucho and da Silva gone?

Then she heard a curious creaking noise. She drew back a veil of leaves and saw, just a few feet away, that a rickety rope bridge had been strung out across the gulf. Two figures were crossing the bridge, one moving quickly and easily, the other, da Silva, clinging on grimly and shuffling forward as if he expected at any moment to be sent plunging into the rushing torrent below.

Now Olly knew what da Silva had been complaining about.

Josh's grimy face appeared next to hers, and the two of them watched from the safety of the trees as da Silva reached the far side of the bridge. Moments later, the jungle had swallowed both men up again.

As soon as they were out of sight, Olly made her way to the rope bridge and examined it dubiously. Ropes as thick as her arm were wound around two wooden pillars set in the ground a few feet from the edge of the ravine. The narrow walkway of planks dipped and rose to the far side — at least thirty feet away. Olly could understand why da Silva had been reluctant to use the bridge. In places, the planks were missing or broken. The whole thing looked old and rotten and ready to fall apart.

She stood on the brink, clinging to the hairy ropes, her heart pounding in her chest as she gingerly took the first step onto the bridge. The plank creaked under her, the ropes rasped and groaned. She looked over her shoulder at Josh. His mouth was set in a thin, determined line.

Holding on with both hands, Olly took a second, cautious step. The rope bridge swayed. Stinging sweat ran into her eyes, but she didn't dare let go to wipe her face. The bridge dipped lower in the middle. Several planks were missing there, and Olly had to take a long step to cross the gap. Below her the rushing water hissed and spat.

Olly felt movement behind her and realized Josh was following her. She began the climb up to the far side. It was steeper than she had anticipated, and a kind of panic began to creep over her. There was a whir by her left ear, and a small, bright blue bird flashed past. Its rapid flight seemed to urge Olly to move more quickly. She was suddenly desperate to get off the bridge — convinced that it was about to fall away beneath her.

But her haste betrayed her. One foot slipped, and Olly came thumping down on her knees, her arms wrenched backward as she clung to the ropes. There was a dry crack, and the plank under her broke. For a moment, she hung in space, supported only by her hands. She saw a shard of rotten wood spiraling down into the water below. Watching it made her feel dizzy. Her fingers started to come loose, and she closed her eyes. She was going to fall.

Then she felt an arm around her waist, and she was dragged backward. She sprawled on the bridge, struggling to breathe.

"Are you OK?" Josh asked.

"Yes," Olly panted. "You can let go now."

She hauled herself to her feet, looking at Josh. "That was close," she breathed.

Josh nodded.

Olly could see by his expression that her accident had scared him. *But not half as much as it scared me*, she thought. "OK," she said firmly. "Let's try that again."

She took a long, careful step over the broken plank. This time there were no mistakes. In a few moments she was on solid ground, holding out her hand to help Josh.

Ahead of them, the jungle stretched out forever. Olly listened for voices. There was nothing.

She stared through the undergrowth. There was no sign of the two men.

She pushed forward through the leaves, her eyes straining for a telltale glimpse of white, her ears alert for any sound of human voices.

A sudden movement on the ground startled her. A long, sinuous yellow shape slithered past and was lost in the undergrowth.

"That was a snake," Josh said under his breath.

"Yes. I know," Olly replied softly.

She pushed on through the forest. "Where are they?" she muttered.

"They couldn't have gone far," Josh replied. "Just keep going straight ahead."

Olly swallowed and nodded. "What if we don't find them?" she asked.

Josh looked at her for a moment, then glanced down at his watch. "Lucho said it was a three-hour march, right?" he said. "Well, we've been walking for nearly three hours now."

"So we should be reaching the Aerie of the White Eagle soon," Olly remarked. "And it's a big outcrop of rock. We ought to be able to find it."

"Let's hope so," Josh responded.

They made their way down into a valley. In front of them, the land folded up in a high ridge.

"Along or up?" Olly asked.

"I think we should go up," Josh said, staring up at the ridge. "We might be able to see something from the top."

They each took a long drink of water, and then began to climb up the hillside. They were a few feet from the top when Olly heard the sound that she had been longing for — a human voice. She couldn't make out the words, but it was a man's voice, speaking sharply, as though issuing orders. She looked at Josh. "It's them!"

Josh frowned. "Is it?" he asked uncertainly. "It doesn't sound like their voices."

"Who else could it be?" Olly asked.

She forced her way to the top of the ridge and peered through the trees. The scene below her took her breath away.

Olly found herself staring across sixty feet of empty air at a man-made structure. It was a huge pyramid, overgrown with dense green foliage. The walls rose in steps to a crowning block that was almost at a level with Olly's line of sight. Lianas, creepers, and other plants covered the entire structure — except for the lower section of the wall facing her, where a dozen or more men were busy clearing the plants away from a monolithic stone entrance. From the square opening spilled a mass of rubble that completely blocked the doorway.

Olly knew exactly what she was looking at: It was an Inca temple, possibly the Lair of the Anaconda King, and the resting place of the Amulet of Quilla. As she stared at it in wonder, the same voice that she had heard before sounded again. She inched herself a little farther forward and stared down the cliff-face.

A man stood on a boulder about thirty-six feet below her. "Steady there," he called. "I want that entrance cleared before dark."

Olly's mind reeled. She knew that voice — and she recognized the man below her.

It was Ethan Cain.

Chapter Twelve: The Inca Temple

"Olly?" Josh called softly to his friend. She was lying full-length on the ground, her head and shoulders above the crest of the hill that overlooked the temple. "Olly? What can you see?"

She didn't reply.

Frowning, Josh crawled up next to her. He soon realized why she hadn't answered.

He stared in stunned silence at the impressive pyramid in front of him. He saw the men working to clear the entrance, hacking and chopping the undergrowth with machetes, then hauling the cut foliage away from the huge stone doorway.

He was still trying to come to terms with this discovery when he saw Benedito da Silva and Lucho, clambering up a mound of white rubble to join a man standing on a large rock. He was watching the workers like a king surveying his armies.

Ethan Cain.

Josh caught his breath in amazement.

Cain's voice drifted up to him. "Da Silva? What

are you doing here?" the voice was sharp and cold — the voice of a man used to giving orders, and used to having them obeyed.

Josh's eyes narrowed — he knew only too well how that voice could change to honey when Ethan wanted to turn on the charm.

Benedito da Silva paused to mop his brow. He was panting, clearly exhausted by the trek through the jungle. "I wanted to see the temple for myself," da Silva replied.

"You don't trust me, is that it?" Ethan asked. "You think I'd take the amulet and not pay you your share?"

Da Silva raised his hands in protest. "I must protect my interests, that is all, Mr. Cain," he said. "Without me, you would not have gotten this far. Did I not find the mantra for you?"

"You were only an errand boy, da Silva," Ethan responded contemptuously. "It was Vargas who found out what Christie was doing. And it was Vargas who made the connection between the carvings on the stone and the old Aymara weavings."

Vargas! Josh remembered the name — Dr. Vargas was the expert that Professor Christie had called in to look at the Puma Punku Stone. So, he had been working for Ethan Cain. That explained a lot.

"But it was I who followed the boy and the girl to the weaver's house and saw the mantra on the wall," da Silva wheedled. "It was I who bought it and brought it to you."

"And you will get your money, once I have the amulet," Cain said dismissively. He turned to Lucho. "Have Christie and Welles been taken for their little walk?"

"Sí, señor," Lucho replied. "They will be gone many days, I think. Sandro knows what you expect of him."

Olly edged backward down the slope, and Josh went with her. They looked at each other. Josh could see fury and dismay in his friend's eyes.

"How did he get here so soon?" Olly hissed.

Josh shrugged. "He probably hired a private plane. He's a millionaire — he can do whatever he likes." He sat on the ground with his head in his hands. "He's really beaten us this time," he went on. "We're on our own, in the middle of the jungle, and he's got a dozen men down there. We can't do a thing to stop him!"

"Oh, no?" Olly demanded. "Well, we're not going to let that rat walk away from here with the Amulet of Quilla. It's not going to happen."

Josh stared at her. "So, what do we do?" he asked.

"We have to get into that temple and find the amulet before Ethan does," Olly said. "Then we have to sneak away again without being seen."

Josh's face lit up. "That's great!" he declared. "So, how do we get into the temple without Ethan knowing about it?"

"I haven't completely figured out that part yet," Olly replied.

Josh looked at her thoughtfully. "You mean you don't have a clue!" he decided.

"You could put it that way, I suppose," Olly admitted.

"We can't do much from here, anyway," Josh pointed out. "Maybe we should make our way around to the other side. That way we can get a lot closer to the pyramid without being seen. If Ethan's men are all concentrating on the front entrance, maybe we can slip in the back door."

Olly stared at him. "Do you think there is one?"

Josh shrugged. "There's only one way to find out," he said.

Olly nodded. "Let's do it."

〰〰

It took them a while to force their way across the hillside and to circle around behind the temple. But eventually, they broke through a curtain of ferns and found themselves right next to it. From there, the ancient building was a lot more imposing. It towered over them, the massive brown stone blocks showing through a green web of creepers and vines and lianas that straggled all the way to the high peak. Beautiful, brilliant blue butterflies pirouetted in the air, their wings the size of Josh's outspread hand.

In the distance they could hear the sounds of the men working. Every so often Ethan Cain's voice would ring out, shouting instructions.

"So?" Olly asked, wiping the sweat out of her eyes. "See a back door?"

Josh stared at the long base wall of the pyramid. It was entirely enveloped in foliage. They would need machetes to hack their way through to the stonework.

"No."

Olly peered up at the side of the Inca temple. "I think I can see holes," she said.

Josh looked up at the stonework.

"See?" Olly said, pointing. "Those dark areas? I think there are some stones missing. Let's climb up and see if we can find a way inside."

They used the thicker branches and creepers for help as they climbed up the first stone step. It was easily twelve feet high. Where patches of stone were visible through the undergrowth, they could see carved patterns and designs. Occasionally a face would stare out from between the leaves and grimace at Josh.

There was a fierce hiss, and Josh drew back in alarm. He had disturbed a large lizard, and it glared fiercely at him with bright eyes before turning its scaly green body and scuttling away.

Eventually, they found themselves standing on the broad platform of the first shelf. They went on to climb the second and third steps of the pyramid — but Josh was tiring rapidly, and he could see that Olly was also exhausted. Of the two bottles of water Josh had brought, one was empty and the other had only a few mouthfuls left.

The sun beat down on them as they stood panting wearily on the fourth step. The climb so far had proved futile. None of the missing stones had revealed a way down into the temple, and Josh was afraid that they were wearing themselves out for nothing.

Olly gazed upward. "Come on," she panted. "We have to keep going."

Josh peeled a large black caterpillar off his arm.

Scores of bright red legs waved as he placed it carefully on a branch. "I think this is a waste of time," he said.

Olly frowned at him, so he shrugged and began to climb again.

Flies whined in Josh's ears and buzzed irritatingly around his face. A large brown spider dropped onto his hand, and he jerked his arm away quickly to dislodge it. The spider fell onto a creeper, but the sleeve of Josh's shirt snagged on a twig. He tugged at it and the cotton ripped, leaving the lower half of his sleeve hanging by a thin strip of material.

"Oh, great!" he groaned, tucking the dangling sleeve up out of the way. He called back to Olly, who was behind him. "Maybe we should give up. We're never going to find a way in like this. Not in a million years."

"No way!" she replied. "If you think —" she broke off with a sudden, startled yelp.

Josh looked over his shoulder. Olly had completely vanished.

"Olly?" Concerned, Josh clambered carefully back down the way he had just come. There was a gap in the foliage. He spread the leaves and saw Olly's grimy face peering up at him from a hole in the stonework. She was clinging to some roots. Josh leaned down and closed his fingers around her wrists.

"I'm OK," she gasped. "There's something under my foot. Just keep hold of me for a second." She twisted and wriggled. "There. I've got it. I'm fine, Josh — you can let go now."

Josh released his grip, and Olly ducked down out of sight.

Curious, Josh kneeled and began clearing the undergrowth away. He saw that Olly had slipped down a wide crack between two of the stone blocks. The crack ran from the edge of the step right in under the next platform. She was bent over, staring down into the hole. Her head bobbed up again — she was grinning.

"Not in a millions years, eh?" Olly laughed. "I can see a way down. Follow me."

She disappeared into the crack again. Josh peered in after her. There was a ledge of stone a few feet down, and then another a little way beyond that. Below him, Olly was clambering lower and lower.

He followed cautiously. The footholds were firm, and once through the heavy roof, Josh was easily able to climb down the half-ruined wall to where Olly was waiting.

"Did you bring your flashlight?" she asked eagerly.

"Of course." Josh put his hand in his pocket and drew out the small pencil-flashlight he always carried. He switched it on, and a thin, bright beam lit the room.

They were in some kind of corridor. The stone floor was traced all over with a carved zigzag design, and the walls, cracked by pale roots and wound about with creepers, were covered in carvings of men and animals. Josh could make out the shapes of scorpions and birds, snakes and pumas, lizards, and other creatures he didn't recognize.

Josh set off along the corridor. The flashlight beam revealed a stone doorway set in the inner wall. He stared into a small, dark chamber while Olly peered over his shoulder. There were no other doorways, and nothing to be seen in the chamber except for the ever-present carvings on the walls and the white roots of creepers that had pushed their way in through the roof and now hung in hairy knots that trailed almost to the floor.

Josh withdrew, and the friends continued along the corridor. They had obviously reached a corner of the pyramid, because the corridor turned sharply to the left before running on straight ahead of them once more. The inner wall was marked by more dark doorways. The second chamber Josh looked into was an exact replica of the first — dark and covered with roots. But the next chamber held a surprise.

It was as dark and creeper-clogged as the others, but beyond the trailing roots, there was a ragged patch of bright light.

Josh and Olly crossed the room to take a closer look.

The far wall of the chamber had a long vertical fracture running down it from roof to floor. Stones had broken and fallen away, and a golden light was spilling in through the gap.

Josh stuck his head through the fissure and gazed into the light. He let out a gasp of sheer amazement.

He was staring down into a huge, lofty chamber, its patterned stone floor about twelve feet below him. It was filled with sunlight that streamed in through cracks in the high roof.

They had reached the heart of the Inca temple.

Chapter Thirteen:
The Lair of the
Anaconda King

Olly pushed in next to Josh so that she could see through the gap. She had expected to see a room on the same level as the one they were in and of a similar scale. When she saw the fabulous chamber at the heart of the pyramid, she was spellbound. Shafts of sunlight pierced the broken roof and made pools of golden light on the geometric designs carved into the floor. The light illuminated what at first appeared to be a lush, exotic garden of rich, green ferns and jewel-bright flowers. But, on closer inspection, Olly realized that the garden was not a deliberate creation but merely the natural result of the jungle's invasion. Green lianas and tumbling vines cascaded from holes in the roof, scattering clusters of fragrant blooms down the walls, in vibrant rainbow colors of red, violet, orange, yellow, and pink. Their scent filled the room, drifting in the bright air and attracting the turquoise butterflies that fluttered from flower to flower.

The chamber itself was oblong, with high walls of dark gray stone that glimmered as though polished. Olly saw a single stone doorway set in the wall at the far end of the chamber. Its mouth was entirely blocked by rubble.

Squat statues lined the walls. They were made out of a greenish stone that glowed in the glorious sunlight. They surrounded a carved rectangle that filled the floor of the room, and their arms stuck out at odd angles, while around their feet — and circling the entire chamber — was a barbed-wire tangle of dry, dead creepers and vines.

"You see what that is, don't you?" Josh said suddenly, pointing down at the patterns that were carved into the floor.

Olly nodded as she looked and recognized the designs. "It's the writing from the Puma Punku Stone!" she exclaimed.

The carvings in the middle of the floor were an exact replica of the Incan symbols on the Puma Punku Stone that told the story of Coyata's flight with the Amulet of Quilla. And the squat, green statues with the curious arms were great sculpted versions of the figures that had filled the border of the stone.

"Have you still got those pictures of the mantra on the camera?" Olly asked.

Josh took the camera out of its pouch and flipped the button to activate it. The small screen on the back lit up. Josh flicked through the stored pictures, until he found the best one of Olly holding the mantra.

The friends peered at the tiny image, their heads together as they tried to make out the details on the photograph.

Olly frowned and looked down into the chamber. "There are the swirly shapes," she said, pointing to one part of the floor. "And there are the squarish parts that look like a maze, and the zigzags, too." She looked at Josh. "It's definitely the same."

Josh shook his head. "The statues are different," he said. He held the camera up close to his eyes. "It's not easy to tell, but I'm sure the positions of the arms aren't the same as they are on the mantra. That's weird."

"The design on the mantra was copied from the Puma Punku Stone." Olly pointed out. "Maybe the people who carved the stone got it wrong." She leaned out of the cleft and peered down. The head of one of the statues was only a few feet below her. "Let's climb down," she said.

"OK," Josh agreed. "Me first."

Olly frowned at him. "Why?"

"Because if I fall, you'll know what *not* to do," Josh told her.

"That's ridiculous!" Olly said, but Josh had already put his flashlight away and was now scrambling through the fissure.

He straddled the wall, reaching down with one leg until his toes just touched the statue's head. He transferred his weight. Olly held onto his collar as he lowered himself carefully onto the statue's broad, flat head.

"OK, let go now," he said.

Olly released him, and Josh crouched down, then turned and eased himself slowly past the statue's face. Olly could see that there were clefts and projections in the statue that made it a fairly easy climb, and it wasn't long before Josh was walking through the crackling dead branches and out into the middle of the chamber and its flourishing garden.

He turned in a long, slow circle, his arms spread out. "Olly! It's amazing!" he called. His voice echoed.

Olly sat astride the broken wall and prepared to follow Josh. "OK," she murmured under her breath. "Here goes." She twisted around, gripping the cracked stonework with both hands and feeling for something solid with her feet.

Josh shouted up to her. "Left a little. That's it. You're almost there." A few moments later, she brought her feet down firmly on the statue's head. She dropped carefully to her knees and stretched one leg down over the huge face. The toe of her shoe lodged safely on a point of carved stone, and Olly lowered herself, reaching for the statue's great upraised arm.

She transferred her weight to the huge stone arm. But then, just as she was about to continue her downward climb, the stone arm began to move.

Olly let out a yell as she felt herself swinging downward. As the statue's arm shifted downward, she completely lost her grip and fell.

She landed on her back in an uncomfortable tangle of dry, spiky branches.

Josh peered down at her. "Are you OK?" he asked.

She hauled herself to her feet and clambered out of the dead undergrowth. "I'm fine," she replied, frowning up at the statue. "That thing deliberately threw me off," she added. "Whose stupid idea was it to make statues with moving arms?"

"I'm not so sure it was a stupid idea," Josh said slowly. "Take a look." He held out the camera for her. "See? Now that the arm has moved, it's in exactly the same position as shown on the mantra and the Puma Punku Stone!"

Olly frowned. "That's odd," she muttered.

A slow grin spread across Josh's face. "It's not odd," he said. "It's brilliant!"

Olly recognized Josh's look of triumph. "OK," she said. "What have you figured out?"

"The pattern on the Puma Punku Stone is the code to finding the Amulet of Quilla," Josh explained excitedly. "The people who built this temple wanted to make sure that no one could get to the amulet without knowing the code — so they built in some safeguards: They put the arms of the statues in the wrong positions."

Olly frowned. "You mean all the statues have moving arms?"

"Exactly," Josh agreed.

"And if we put them in the right positions — somehow that will lead us to the amulet?"

"Yes."

Olly looked around. Fourteen of the great squat

statues lined the walls of the chamber: one in each corner, three on the long walls, and two along the shorter walls. Rearranging all those arms was going to take some time.

Olly jogged over to the wall and listened. She could hear distant, muffled sounds — the unmistakeable thud, crash, and rumble of rocks being moved.

She ran back to where Josh was standing, peering at the camera. "We don't have much time," she said. "I'll climb the statues, you call out the positions the arms should be in." She looked anxiously over her shoulder at the entranceway. "And let's hope we get it done before Ethan Cain's men break through."

~~~~~

It was not an easy task to adjust the arms on all the statues, and nearly half an hour had passed by the time Olly reached the final green figure. Josh could see that she was worn out, but there was no time to rest — the sharp sounds echoing from the entranceway were getting louder all the time. Ethan Cain's men might appear at any minute.

"OK," Olly called down breathlessly. "What do I move?"

"The left arm should be twisted downward," Josh instructed. He watched as Olly climbed the statue until she could reach its raised left arm. She tried to tug it down. Nothing happened.

Josh heard a loud noise from the entrance. Cain's men were getting close. They were running out of time.

"It won't move," Olly panted. "It's stuck."

"It's the last one, Olly," Josh urged. "Give it another try."

Olly sighed. "I'll . . . try . . . something . . . else . . ." she gasped. She climbed higher and stood precariously on the statue's narrow shoulder. Hanging on to its head as best she could, she kicked at the arm.

There was a grating sound. Olly kicked again. The arm rotated suddenly and came sweeping down.

Josh stared at the mantra on the camera screen. Yes! Now all the statues were positioned exactly as they were on the weaving copied from the Puma Punku Stone.

Olly was looking around hopefully. "Well?" she called. "Now what?"

"I don't know," Josh replied. And then he heard a low rumble.

He looked over his shoulder, assuming that the sound had come from the entrance. But then he realized that it was coming from the floor beneath his feet. He felt the stones vibrate under his shoes. "Uh, Olly . . ." he breathed, staring down at the quivering floor. "Something's happening!"

A moment later, the rumbling became a loud grinding noise as the floor began to disappear from underneath Josh. He threw himself backward, falling full length on the ground. The massive stones in the very center of the room were pivoting and falling away to leave a large square gap. Josh pushed himself frantically away from the hole with his heels.

As he watched in amazement, a gigantic snake came thrusting up out of the gap. It was yellow, its back and sides spotted with black, its eyes bright, its scales gleaming. It reared over Josh, its mouth open and fangs bared, as if about to strike.

For a terrifying moment, Josh thought it was real, but then he realized that the scales were carved from shining yellow stone, and the powerful head was fixed in position.

The dust of centuries rained down from the massive stone snake as it quivered for a moment. Then all was still again.

Josh got to his feet, his heart hammering. He stared up dizzily at the huge snake. There was something very majestic about the arch of its neck and its glittering black eyes. But, most impressive of all, on top of its head was a huge, faceted crystal that caught the sunshine streaming in through the roof and sent brilliant beams of light scattering in every direction.

This, Josh realized, was the Anaconda King.

〰〰

Olly was nearly sent tumbling from her perch on the statue's shoulder, as the middle of the floor opened up and the monstrous snake rose into the chamber. She clung on for dear life as the great stones of the temple shuddered and shook.

And then the room was still again. Olly stared, speechless, as dust filtered down through the air and daggers of light stabbed out from the jewel on the snake's head, raking the chamber.

"Josh?" she called down, after a moment. "Are you OK?"

"Yes," he replied. "Olly, look! *Look!*"

He was staring at the walls. Between the statues in the two longest walls, square entrances had opened up — two in each wall.

Heedless of falling, Olly scrambled down the statue and ran out onto what remained of the floor.

Each of the entrances was made up of four doorways, one inside the other — leading about six feet deep into the walls. Then there was nothing but a blank wall of smooth-set stonework. They were exactly the same as the niches they had seen on the Island of the Moon — the niches in the walls of Inak Uyu.

But here there was a symbol set into the facade of each door — a sun with eight rays radiating from it, a crescent moon, a five-pointed star, the face of a puma.

As Olly gazed in awe at the massive doorways, she was only half-aware of faint smoke beginning to rise from the dried creepers that surrounded the room. The dead vegetation was smoldering in the fierce beams of focused sunlight that darted from the crystal crown of the Anaconda King.

"What do we do now?" Josh asked.

"We have to choose which doorway will lead us to the amulet," Olly breathed. "And fast."

A sudden rumbling sounded from behind them. They both turned in time to see a cloud of dust billow out from the entrance tunnel. And then they heard a voice shouting, "I see light! Stand back there — let me through."

Olly and Josh looked at each other in horror.

"It may be dangerous," called the voice. "Keep back till I call."

Stones spilled out of the entrance, rattling on the temple floor. And then a figure emerged from the dust. Ethan Cain came scrambling down the rubble and into the chamber with a look of triumphant delight on his face.

They had not been fast enough, Olly thought in despair, their enemy had broken through.

Chapter Fourteen: A Leap of Faith

Olly and Josh watched miserably as the man clambered through the tangle of dried branches and strode out into the chamber. He was smiling, and his eyes shined with greed. For several seconds he didn't notice the friends.

"Hello, Mr. Cain," Olly said wearily.

The smile vanished from Ethan's face in an instant, to be replaced by a look of disbelief — of utter astonishment. But he swallowed the shock quickly, and his face hardened.

"Olly and Josh," he remarked. "You never cease to astound me."

A sharp crackling interrupted their conversation. In several places, the smoldering branches had burst into flame under the intense heat of the light beams coming from the Anaconda King's crystal crown. Smoke was rising up the walls, and the fire was spreading rapidly, the flames running swiftly along the tangle of dead branches.

Ethan Cain stared around the walls. "Where is the amulet?" he shouted, his voice shrill with panic.

"We don't know," Josh yelled.

"And we wouldn't tell you if we did!" Olly added.

Ethan Cain ran into the middle of the chamber, his eyes scanning the walls. "Four sacred niches," he hissed. "Sun — moon — star — animal. But which one holds the amulet?" He glared up at the carved symbols, and then a fierce grin spread across his face. "Of course, Quilla was the goddess of the moon!" he exclaimed in delight.

He bounded across the chamber, kicking and dragging the smoldering branches away from the niche with the moon symbol.

The flames were leaping all around the chamber now. A wall of hissing and spitting fire completely blocked the entranceway so recently cleared of rubble.

But Ethan had managed to clear a narrow path through the dead branches. He stamped out the few flames that licked around the gap. Then, with a final victorious glance at Olly and Josh, he stepped through the opening he had made and approached the niche.

Walking in under the four stepped doorways, he stood facing the solid wall of stones and spread his hands out over the blocks, running his fingers over them carefully.

Josh started to run toward him, as if he hoped to somehow stop Ethan. But Olly caught hold of his arm and held him back.

"Let him try," she said quietly. "I think he's got it wrong."

Josh stared at her in confusion.

"Just watch!" Olly told him. Her eyes were focused intently on the man as he examined the stones. She remembered the legend that Beatriz had told them — of the puma that had led Coyata to the temple. She felt certain that the crescent moon symbol would not lead to the Amulet of Quilla — the puma was the guide.

She saw Ethan's hands come to rest on a single point in the wall. He seemed to press something, and Olly saw one of the stones slide away to reveal a gaping hole. She caught her breath, suddenly filled with doubt. Ethan had found something! Was it that simple? Did the doorway of the crescent moon really lead to the lost Amulet of Quilla?

The answer came swiftly and suddenly.

As Ethan reached into the hole, a slab of stone

came sliding down behind him, shutting the niche off — and imprisoning him inside.

Josh let out a gasp of shock as the stone block came crashing down — and Olly heaved a sigh of relief.

Josh broke free from Olly's grip and ran toward the gap in the wall of flaming branches. Apart from that one gap, the fire completely encircled the chamber now, the flames licking and dancing around the shoulders of the impassive statues.

Olly ran after Josh. He was already at the niche, pressing his ear to the stone. "Mr. Cain? Are you all right?" he called. Josh hadn't noticed the small oblong cavity in the face of the stone. It was at waist height.

Olly kneeled and put her mouth to the hole. "Can you hear me?" she asked.

Quick as a striking snake, Ethan's arm shot out of the hole and his fingers clenched Olly's throat.

"Get me out of here!" Ethan bellowed. "Call my men!"

Olly couldn't speak — the fingers were choking her. She clawed at Ethan's wrist, trying desperately to pry his fingers off.

Then Josh's fist suddenly came hammering down on the disembodied forearm. "Let her go!" he yelled, battering at Ethan's arm.

The fingers lost their grip and Olly scrambled away.

"Did he hurt you?" Josh asked as he helped her up.

Olly touched her neck. It was a little bit sore, but otherwise intact. "No, I'm fine," she replied.

She turned and ran back through the breach in the wall of flames. "Ethan's men will get him out of there as soon as the fire dies down," she said. She looked at Josh. "He's safe enough for now. We have to find the amulet."

Josh stared at her in disbelief. "Look at this place, Olly!" he shouted. "We're surrounded by fire. We can't get at any of the other doorways, even if we knew which was the right one."

Olly smiled. She felt curiously calm and clear-headed. "Remember that old legend Beatriz told us?" she said.

Josh frowned. "Yes — why?"

"Coyata went into a valley," Olly reminded him. "And there was a wall of flames blocking her way. She was going to turn back, but her puma guide led her on through the fire."

"Yes, I remember," Josh agreed in confusion. "But . . ."

Olly turned and pointed to the niched door with

the symbol of the puma set in it. The golden face was just visible, shining brightly in the leaping flames. "That's where the Amulet of Quilla is hidden," she said quietly.

"But we can't reach it," Josh argued. He stared into the roaring wall of flame and frowned. "How is that stuff burning so fiercely anyway?" he asked. "It's just a lot of dried twigs — it should have burned away to nothing by now."

"Maybe it's not an ordinary fire," Olly suggested.

"I think you're right," Josh agreed, his eyes opening wide. "I think these branches were put here on purpose. It's some kind of booby trap. They were probably treated with some kind of chemical to make them burn longer."

"The puma led Coyata through the flames," Olly murmured, taking a step closer to the wall of fire. Her eyes were fixed on the shimmering golden puma face behind the leaping flames.

"That was just a legend," Josh said. "We have to wait till the fire goes out."

Olly didn't turn away from the puma. "Cain's men will be able to get in here then," she replied. "We can't wait that long." She took another step toward the flames.

"What choice do we have?" Josh asked desperately.

Olly bit her lip, summoning her courage. It wasn't logical — it made no real sense — but somehow she knew that she had to go through the flames.

She remembered the shard of pottery with the puma face on it that she had found at the bottom of Lake Titicaca. She remembered Beatriz's voice as she had told the legend of Coyata and her puma guide. She fixed her gaze on the carved puma face above the massive stone niche. And then she ran forward and leaped into the flames.

〰〰

Josh let out a horrified yell as Olly jumped. For a moment, she seemed to hang in the air, engulfed by the hungry flames. And then she was through. He saw her land lightly and turn toward him, her slim shape seeming to twist and writhe as the fire danced between them.

"Olly?" he called.

"It's fine, Josh," she shouted back to him. "Come through. You won't get burned."

Josh stared at her. It was impossible. He could feel the terrible heat of the flames already.

"What are you waiting for?" There was something wonderfully normal in the impatient tone of

Olly's voice. "Are you going to help me find the amulet, or are you just going to stand there?"

Josh let out a gasp of amazed laughter. "OK, OK," he said. "I'm coming."

He backed off a few paces, trying not to think about the impossibility of what he had just seen — and of what he was about to do. He rocked on his heels. "Three . . . two . . . one . . . go!" he yelled, and ran at the flames.

He leaped high. The fire was all around him. The heat was terrible. His head swam. And then he was through the flames.

Olly looked at him. She was smiling. "Easy, wasn't it?"

Josh gazed at the barrier of fire and then at his smiling friend. The flames were dancing in Olly's eyes. "How did you know it would be safe?" he asked.

"I didn't *know*," Olly told him. "But I remembered what Beatriz said — that the five hundred years of darkness would soon come to an end — that it was time for the amulet to be found." She looked sharply at him. "Don't you dare laugh at me, Josh, but I think we're meant to find the amulet."

Josh simply shook his head and shrugged. He didn't know what to say.

Olly turned and walked through the doorway until she reached the flat stone wall at the back. She ran her hands over the stone as Ethan had done. Josh joined her, and together they felt for something that might open a way through.

Olly pressed against each stone block, and found one that moved slightly. She pushed more firmly, and it slid back with a small grating sound. She reached into the gap. And then, with a much louder grating sound, the whole wall opened up in front of them — splitting down the center, from floor to lintel, and sliding apart to let the friends through.

"Can I have your flashlight?" Olly asked.

Wordlessly, Josh took it from his pocket and handed it to her.

The thin, white beam illuminated a small, dark chamber, no more than nine feet square. The walls were green with lichen and moss. Lying in the middle of the chamber was a casket of polished black stone about three feet long, and half that wide. It was carved all over with Incan designs.

Olly walked into the chamber and knelt before the casket. She grasped the lid and tried to lift it. It wouldn't budge.

She looked over her shoulder at Josh. "Help me," she groaned. "It's heavy."

Josh went around to the other side of the box and grasped the cold stone lid. They heaved and it came open a crack. Josh heaved again, putting all his strength into the effort. The lid rose and fell back.

But, as it did so, with a great rumble, the door crashed shut again, sealing them inside the chamber.

Josh stared at it in horror. "We're trapped," he gasped.

Olly stared at the wall that had once been a door. "We came here to find the Amulet of Quilla, Josh," she said, her voice strangely calm. "We'll worry about getting out once we've found it." She shined the flashlight into the stone casket. "Is this silver, do you think?"

There was another box inside the first that did indeed appear to be made of silver. Its lid was finely etched with stylized animals — llamas, lizards, hummingbirds, eagles, dogs, monkeys — there were scores of them, all grouped around representations of the moon in its various stages from crescent to full.

"It's amazing," Josh said, gazing at the beautiful engraving. "How did they do all this?"

"I don't know," Olly replied. "But I bet it took ages! Can you help me lift it out?"

The box had handles on both sides. It was heavy, but together the friends managed to pull it up and out of the stone casket. They set it down on the floor. There was no lock, so Olly lifted the lid and shined the flashlight inside.

The light played over another box. This one was made from some kind of white crystalline stone that sent sparks of light dancing across the roof and walls of the chamber.

Olly gasped in wonder, and Josh saw that the crystal was covered in carvings of pumas. The beautiful animals were shown in various positions — some running and leaping, others sitting or lying with their paws outstretched. He leaned forward to look more closely. The detail was incredible — the pumas even had tiny, needlelike claws and whiskers.

Olly reached in carefully and pulled out the crystal box.

Josh crouched by her side, and together they opened the lid. The casket inside was a rich yellow gold that burned with a deep luster as the beam of the flashlight ran over it. The box was a few feet long, and covered with more of the fine etchings — this time of simple spirals, triangles, stars, and squares, and series of parallel lines that Josh recognized as ladders.

"Ladders have something to do with death," Josh murmured. "I remember reading about it. Maybe we shouldn't open this one, Olly — we might not like what we find inside."

Olly looked at him. "I'm not giving up now!" she said. Silently, she lifted the lid of the golden casket — and let out a yell of shock and dismay!

Josh looked inside with curiosity, and shuddered. There was a dried, withered arm resting on a cushion of reeds. It was quite small and slender — Josh guessed it was a woman's arm. The skin was as brown as old leather and shrunken to reveal the shapes of the bones beneath. But the fingers were curled like dry, brown twigs around a crescent-shaped amulet of bright gold. It was covered with engravings and inlaid with diamonds and emeralds and rubies and sapphires that sparkled magnificently in the flashlight beam.

Olly smiled at Josh, her face patterned with a rainbow of colored lights reflected from the jewels. "We've found the Amulet of Quilla!" she breathed in awe.

Josh nodded, realizing that it was true. He was looking at the Amulet of Quilla, held in the shriveled hand of Quilla's loyal handmaiden, Coyata.

He reached into the casket, and jumped in

surprise as the bony fingers snapped open. His heart pounding, he lifted the amulet out of Coyata's hand. It felt heavy — heavier than he had expected from such a delicate object.

A small, sharp click sounded from the far end of the chamber. Olly shined the flashlight at the wall, and they saw that a stone near the floor had slid aside to reveal a dark passageway.

"That must be our way out," Olly remarked softly.

Josh nodded. "We should wrap up the amulet," he said. "To keep it safe." He tore off the ripped sleeve of his shirt and carefully wrapped the amulet in it, watching as the fabric smothered the spinning rainbows of light. Then he slipped the precious package into his shoulder bag. "Let's get out of here," he said.

They kneeled at the entrance of the tunnel and peered inside. The passage was narrow — only just wide and high enough for them to crawl through.

Josh took his flashlight back from Olly and, on all fours, crawled in under the wall. He aimed the flashlight ahead and saw that the square, stone tunnel ran straight ahead for as far as he could see. There was no light at the end, and no suggestion of how far it went.

Josh crawled silently on along the tunnel with Olly following. It was cool, but airless and stifling. Olly didn't say anything, but Josh knew that she must feel the same as he did — there would be no celebrations until they were safely out of the Inca pyramid.

The tunnel dipped at a shallow angle, and Josh guessed it was taking them beneath the massive temple walls. But a little while later, the tunnel showed no sign of finishing, and Josh became puzzled. "We can't still be under the temple," he panted. "We've come too far."

"We still have to keep going," Olly said. "What other choice do we have?"

She was right, of course — they had to follow the tunnel to its end, but Josh was beginning to wonder where exactly that end might be. And a more disturbing thought had occurred to him — did the architects of the ancient temple have any more tricks in store for them? So far, they had passed every test, but what if the tunnel was the final trap — what if it led nowhere?

The tunnel began to narrow alarmingly, and then they came to a place where it widened and split in two. Josh stopped and sat back on his heels, playing the flashlight beam along both channels. The tunnel to the right was by far the wider of the two. The left-hand one was tiny by comparison, and its sides and roof were jagged so that it looked like the open mouth of a hungry animal. The only way through that cramped entrance would be for them to lie flat and wriggle along on their bellies, squeezing in under the stone teeth.

And there was something else that Josh noticed: the stone teeth were angled inward down the throat of the tunnel, like the teeth of a predator, allowing prey in, but preventing escape.

Josh started forward toward the larger, right-hand tunnel. Olly didn't follow. He turned and looked at her. "This must be the way," he said.

"No, I don't think so," she disagreed. "Look." She took the flashlight and pointed it at a spot just above the entrance to the smaller tunnel. The pool of light picked out a carving on the stone that Josh hadn't noticed before. It was the face of a puma.

Josh frowned. "But we can't go through there," he said.

"The puma has led us this far," Olly pointed out. "It won't send us the wrong way now."

Josh stared at her. She looked tired — but there was a determined light in her eyes. "Are you absolutely sure?" he asked.

"Yes. This is the right way," Olly declared firmly. "Trust the puma, Josh."

He watched as Olly flattened herself on the ground and squeezed into the tunnel. Slowly, her body slid into the hungry mouth. The flashlight beam faded, and Josh found himself in absolute darkness. He could hear Olly's breathing, and the scrabbling noise of her body edging deeper into the tunnel.

Josh sighed and felt his way to the mouth of the left-hand tunnel. He stretched out and crawled in after Olly. Stone teeth scraped his shoulders and head. He stopped for a moment and tried backing out of the passage, but the stone teeth snagged in his clothes, stopping him.

"You had better be right about this, Olly," Josh muttered under his breath as he began to edge forward again. "Because if you're wrong, there's no way back."

Chapter Fifteen: ⌒
The End of Darkness

Olly dragged herself along the tunnel, grazed by the sharp stones that pressed in all around her. She had entered the narrow stone passage, driven by the absolute conviction that the puma would always lead her the right way, and that she and Josh were somehow *meant* to find the amulet. But as the tunnel burrowed on and on, growing no wider and showing no sign of reaching an end, her faith began to wane. Could she have been wrong? The significance of the angled stone teeth had dawned on her, too. If she *was* wrong, she had led them into a deadly trap from which there could be no escape.

And then a new problem appeared. The flashlight shined on dangling roots that began to clog the tunnel, making progress even more arduous. Olly pushed on, but the pale, hairy roots crowded in around her, smelling ripe and feeling unpleasantly soft.

She paused, fighting for breath, taking a moment

or two to gather her strength for another push forward. She felt Josh at her feet.

His voice came up to her in a muffled croak. "What's wrong?"

Olly took a deep breath. "Nothing," she replied, trying to ignore her doubts and fears and struggle on. But the flashlight was shining on a tangle of pale vegetation ahead that almost completely blocked the tunnel. Roots bent and snapped as Olly dragged herself past them — but there were so many ahead that she feared they would form an impenetrable barrier.

For a moment she despaired completely. They would never get through. They would die in this terrible tunnel, their bodies would never be found, and it would be *all her fault*.

But as her spirits reached their lowest ebb, she suddenly realized that she could see a faint green light ahead — and it had nothing to do with her flashlight.

The foliage that was blocking the way wasn't just more of the sickly white roots — it was green and lush, with leaves and curling green tendrils. Olly gave a sound that was half-gasp, half-shout and heaved herself into the dense barrier of greenery.

Her head emerged into bright sunlight. It dazzled her, and for a few moments she was totally disoriented. The ground seemed to be missing, and all she could see was a blur of brown that seemed to dance in the air many feet in front of her. She blinked and rubbed her eyes, and suddenly everything snapped into focus.

Olly gasped. The ground *was* missing — it fell away in a cliff-face. And thirty feet below, the foaming white waters of a narrow stream leaped and crashed over knife-sharp rocks. The brown in front of her was the far wall of the gorge, topped with trees and sprawling ferns and alive with blue and red butterflies.

Directly beneath her, Olly saw that a ledge had been cut into the rock-face. She wriggled carefully out of the tunnel and stood on the narrow shelf, leaning back against the cliff. She could see the ledge snaking its way slowly down to the rushing water below. A treachorous path, but a path just the same.

Josh's grimy face appeared through the greenery covering the mouth of the tunnel beside her. Olly helped him to crawl out, and they both stood in silence for a few moments, just relishing the sunlight, the clear, fresh air, and the sound of the racing water.

"Do you know what's really strange about the last part of that tunnel — the section after the split?" Josh said at last.

Olly looked at him. "What?"

"It's too narrow for an adult to get through," Josh told her. "And that's strange, because it means no adult could ever have escaped with the amulet."

Olly turned her head to look along the cliff-face. About nine feet to the right of where they were standing, there was a black cleft in the rock. She pointed at it. "I think that's the mouth of the other tunnel," she said.

Josh nodded. "You see, there's no ledge there, no path," he pointed out. "And it's too far away for anyone to climb from there to here. Anyone who chose that tunnel would be stuck. There's no way up. And no way down unless they jumped."

"You couldn't jump from this height," Olly said. "You'd be killed."

"Yes," Josh agreed.

"Is the amulet safe?" Olly asked eagerly.

Josh took the folded bundle out of his bag and carefully unwrapped it. The golden crescent moon glittered and gleamed. It was far more beautiful in the bright sunlight, where the jewels blazed like colored fire.

Olly touched it gently. "Put it away," she said, her voice soft and reverent. She turned her head and stared across the ravine. "Now we have to get back to Rurre," she murmured. "If we can."

Josh grinned. "I have an idea about that," he said. He pointed down to the rushing water. "I think that if we follow the stream, it will lead us to the Rio Beni. And then we can follow that out of the jungle!"

They followed the ledge down to the noisy white water. Near the bank, the stream was only ankle deep, and it wasn't difficult for the two of them to pick their way over the slippery rocks. Gradually the stream widened and calmed, so that the friends were sometimes picking their way over dry stones, and sometimes walking on mud-banks.

They saw an iguana sprawling on the brown rocks, basking in the afternoon sun. Sandflies danced wildly in swarms over the water, and the frogs watched them hungrily from wet hollows. The air was full of butterflies and the sound of monkeys chattering in the treetops.

Olly almost stepped on a salamander. "Sorry!" she said, watching as it slipped into the water and made off across the stream, leaving wide ripples in its wake. She saw movement farther downstream. "Look," she said. "Fish." There was a whole shoal of them. They were about twelve inches long, and their gray backs shined like polished steel under the clear water. Their heads were large and blunt.

Josh peered at the fish suspiciously. "Piranhas!" he declared after a moment. "I wouldn't try making friends — they'd eat you alive."

"Oh!"

After an hour or so, the steep banks of the stream began to broaden and fall away. Soon, the friends were walking along a rocky shoreline under tall trees.

Olly was thoughtful. She looked at Josh. "I guess Ethan's men will have rescued him by now," she said. "It won't take him long to realize we've got the amulet — not once he takes a look in that room with all the boxes." She frowned. "I wonder what he'll do."

"He'll go crazy," Josh said with a grin. "And I wish I was there to see it."

"Me, too," Olly agreed. "But what are we going to tell everyone? We know that Dr. Vargas and Mr. da Silva and Sandro were all working for Ethan — but you know what he's like. He'll find a way of making it all sound completely innocent."

Josh nodded. "It'll be our word against his," he said. "Jonathan and the others will think we've got it all wrong."

"We've found the Amulet of Quilla," Olly sighed. "That's the most important thing." She gave a growl of frustration. "But we still can't prove Ethan is a rat. If we try, it'll only get us in more trouble." She sighed again and thought for a few moments. "We'll tell them we overheard someone saying that there was a rocky outcrop near town known as Eagle's Nest. And we thought it might be the Aerie of the White Eagle — so we went to check it out. We'll say we found the temple, and Ethan and his gang were already there — but we got to the amulet first." She looked at Josh. "And we'll leave everything else out, right?"

Josh nodded.

"But one day," Olly added, "we'll find some way of proving what Ethan's *really* like."

Josh smiled grimly. "Yes, we will," he agreed fervently. "But not today."

The friends followed the stream for another half an hour, and then they found themselves standing on the banks of the great Rio Beni. The river curved away from them in a wide loop. Fingers of white mist curled out of the jungle and hovered over the glimmering water. The sun was low and red in the sky behind them. It was nearly six o'clock.

"How far do you think it is to Rurre?" Olly asked. "Gran will worry if we're not back soon."

"I don't know," Josh said. He pointed to the right. "But I think it must be that way."

They began to walk along the riverbank, feeling tired but happy. They had found the long lost Amulet of Quilla — Olly just wished they didn't have such a long walk home.

And she was in luck; they had only been stumbling along beside the Rio Beni for a few minutes when a canoe glided into sight through the silvery evening mist. They waved and shouted. The man in the canoe spotted them and grinned. He turned the boat and paddled toward them.

〰〰

Olly leaned back in the prow of the canoe, delighted to be able to rest at last and watch the jungle slip past. Josh sat facing her, looking along the river in the direction they were traveling.

Their rescuer was gazing out over their heads, his arms working smoothly as he paddled. Olly closed her eyes, listening to the steady splash of the paddle. She trailed her fingers in the cool water.

"Piranha!" Josh cried suddenly.

Olly sat up with a jerk, snatching her hand out of the water and peering over the side of the boat in alarm. There was no sign of any fish — let alone piranhas.

Olly looked at Josh — he was grinning. She laughed and flicked water at him.

But Josh was momentarily distracted by something else.

Olly looked over her shoulder. Around a long curve, she could see buildings spilling down to the shoreline.

They had reached Rurre.

It was only a few minutes later that Olly and Josh were climbing wearily up the steps of the hacienda, relieved that their long adventure was almost at an end.

"Good heavens — look at the state of you!" said a familiar voice.

Olly looked around to see her grandma sitting on the veranda with a magazine, a drink, and a horrified expression on her face.

"Gran — you're up," Olly remarked happily. "Are you feeling better?"

"I was until I saw the two of you," her grandma replied. "What on earth have you been up to?

You're absolutely filthy." Her eyes narrowed. "You've been in the jungle, haven't you? And I specifically told you —"

Olly held up her hands. "Before you yell at us, Gran," she said. "Can I just say it was for a really good cause? And you'll be pleased when we explain it all — but could we have a drink first? Our water ran out hours ago and we're really thirsty."

Audrey Beckmann held out her glass. Olly half-drained the cool mango juice in one long gulp, then passed the glass on to Josh. He finished it.

"Now then," Mrs. Beckmann said. "Would one of you like to explain exactly why you decided to go into the jungle when I expressly asked you not to? You look as if you've been wallowing in mud like a pair of hippos."

"Well," Josh began. "It's a long story. You see . . ." His voice trailed off as a new figure emerged from the house.

Olly's eyes widened in surprise. "Jonathan?" she said, staring at Josh's brother. "What are you doing back?"

"We had some back luck," Jonathan told her. "I don't want you to worry — everything's under control — but your father was bitten by a snake."

"Where is he?" Olly gasped.

"He's lying down in his room," Jonathan replied. "But . . ."

Olly didn't wait to hear any more. Her father was hurt! She sprang through the door, ran up the stairs three at a time, and burst into his room.

Professor Christie was in bed, propped up on pillows and busy making notes on a sheaf of documents that spilled over the sheets. "Olivia!" he gasped as she came flying across the room. "Look at your clothes! What in the world have you been up to?"

She flung her arms around his neck. "Are you OK?" she panted. "Jonathan said you got bitten by a snake. Was it poisonous? Have you seen a doctor?" She frowned at him, her voice full of fear and concern. "How could you let yourself get bitten by a snake?"

Her father hugged her. "Calm down, Olivia," he said. "I'm perfectly all right. Katerina called a doctor, and he's examined the bite. The snake wasn't poisonous, and I'll be fit as a fiddle in no time. We only came back because Jonathan insisted."

"Yes, I did," Jonathan said, coming into the room. "We didn't know how serious it might have been."

Josh and Mrs. Beckmann followed him in.

"I think your father could do with some peace and quiet," said Olly's grandma. "And he certainly doesn't need you covering him in mud, Olivia."

Olly sat back and looked at Josh. "Show them," she said.

Josh took the precious bundle out of his bag and slowly unwrapped it. The sparkling jewels sent rainbows of light flying around the white walls.

"It's the Amulet of Quilla," Josh said, reverently holding it up for everyone to see.

Papers cascaded to the floor as Professor Christie leaped out of bed. He limped over to Josh and carefully took the amulet out of his hand. Jonathan and Audrey Beckmann stared over Josh's shoulder, their eyes filled with amazement.

"Where did you find it?" the professor breathed.

"In the Lair of the Anaconda King," Olly said proudly. "Ethan Cain was already there, but we beat him to it!"

Jonathan, Mrs. Beckman, and Professor Christie looked even more confused.

"Ethan Cain?" the professor queried. "Olivia — what are you talking about?"

"You should sit down, Dad," Olly told him firmly. "It's quite a story!"

It was nearly seven o'clock that same evening. Everyone was out on the veranda. The professor had his leg propped up on a spare chair. Olly and Josh had showered and changed clothes. And they were all digging in to a delicious meal that Katerina had provided for them.

Jonathan was examining the amulet with an eye-piece and making copies of the intricate engravings in a notebook.

Olly looked up as a figure suddenly rushed out of the trees toward the veranda. It was Ethan Cain.

Everyone stared at him in surprise. Olly could hardly believe her eyes — the handsome business-man showed no signs of his ordeal in the jungle. His clothes were clean and smart, and he bounded up the stairs as though full of energy.

At first, his face was filled with anxiety. But then he caught sight of Olly and Josh, and a look of abso-lute astonishment replaced the concern. "Josh! Olly! You're here!" he gasped. "That's such a relief! I was afraid you'd got lost in the jungle. Why did you run off like that? What happened to you?"

It was such a perfect act, Olly could almost have fallen for it herself — if she hadn't known Ethan Cain as well as she did.

Professor Christie stood up to greet him. "Olivia and Josh told us they met you in the jungle, Ethan," he said, limping forward and shaking the American's hand. "But I don't understand — what are you doing here? Jonathan told me you'd been forced to break off your vacation with Natasha to deal with a work crisis in California."

Ethan Cain nodded. "That's exactly what happened," he confirmed. "But things were nowhere near as bad as I'd been led to believe. In fact, by the time I got to California, the whole thing had blown over." He smiled. "It was too late to travel all the way back to Australia, so I decided to come and see how you were getting along with your search for the Amulet of Quilla." He smiled at Josh. "Your e-mail to Natasha made it sound as if you were really on to something." He looked at Professor Christie. "Then I had some real luck. I met up with a local guide who knew of an Incan temple hidden in the jungle not far from here. It's an amazing place." He gestured to Olly and Josh. "These two can tell you all about it. They got there ahead of me." He grinned. "I take it you did find the Amulet of Quilla?" he asked.

The professor picked up the golden amulet and held it out. Ethan Cain took it carefully in both hands. Olly saw greed and desire shining briefly in his eyes.

"Marvelous!" he said softly. "It's even more beautiful that I'd imagined." He put the amulet down, his fingers lingering on the surface for a few moments, as if he could not bring himself to let it go. Then he turned and Olly saw that he wore his usual charming, guileless smile. "I think we should celebrate," he declared. "I would like you all to join me at the Hotel Safari tonight. Olly and Josh will be the guests of honor!"

~~~~

It was, of course, the best hotel in Rurrenabaque. Ethan Cain had taken a luxurious apartment with a balcony overlooking the Rio Beni. The western horizon glowed with the last few threads of purple light, and a full moon was riding high in the velvet sky, making the river mists gleam like silver. The jungle spread out around them, dark and mysterious.

Ethan stood on the wide balcony with his guests, pouring champagne into their glasses. Mrs. Beckmann had given Olly and Josh orange juice for the toast.

"To the Amulet of Quilla," Ethan Cain said, raising his glass. He looked at Olly, and for a moment she caught, deep in his eyes, a flash of anger and resentment that sent a chill up her spine. "And to Olly and Josh for finding it!" Ethan finished.

Everyone drank.

"I'd like to make a toast, too," Olly said, her eyes resting defiantly on the American. "Here's to my dad, and here's to him finding the next Talisman of the Moon."

She watched as Ethan Cain drank the toast. He put the glass to his lips and drank heartily without a glimmer of annoyance.

"This is the third time we've beaten him," Olly whispered to Josh. "He must be furious, but you wouldn't know it by looking at him."

Josh stared at the suave businessman. "He is smooth," he growled under his breath. "How else would he be able to fool my mom the way he does?"

"We'll find a way to prove what he's really like," Olly said. "Look at him now, sweet-talking my dad! I bet he's already planning how to get his hands on the next talisman. But we're on to him. Ethan Cain had better watch out."

The two friends moved to one end of the balcony. Olly leaned on the rail, gazing down into the jungle. A subtle movement caught her eye. A long dark shape was padding out of the trees and slipping silently down toward the river.

Olly caught her breath. "Josh, look!" she breathed.

The sinuous, dark animal was at the river's edge now. As they watched, it lowered its head to drink.

"What is it?" Josh whispered as he peered into the gloom.

Can't you see?" Olly replied, her eyes shining. "It's a puma!"

At that moment, the beautiful creature lifted its head — and Olly could have sworn that it looked straight up at her — before it turned and stalked majestically back into the unfathomable jungle.

ON THE RUN

TWO FUGITIVE KIDS.
ONE BIG MISSION. THE CHASE IS ON!

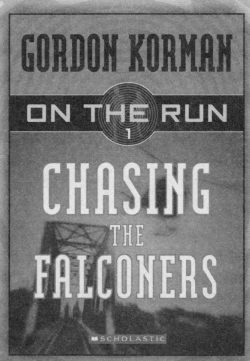

The Falconers are facing life in prison—unless their children, Aiden and Meg, can follow a trail of clues to prove their parents' innocence. Aiden and Meg are on the run, and they must use their wits to make it across the country, facing plenty of risks along the way!

■SCHOLASTIC

OTRT

WISHING FOR MORE THRILLING ADVENTURES?

Children of the Lamp
The Akhenaten Adventure
by P. B. Kerr

Join powerful djinn twins John and Philippa and their eccentric uncle Nimrod on a magical ride to locate a monstrous pharaoh.

Chasing Vermeer
by Blue Balliett

When a priceless Vermeer painting vanishes, two friends find themselves deciphering clues in the middle of an international art scandal, where everyone is suspect.

The Thief Lord
by Cornelia Funke

A magical thriller set among the canals of Venice, where two runaway orphan brothers join a ring of street children led by the mysterious Thief Lord.

■SCHOLASTIC

www.scholastic.com

FILLLADVN1